Seduced

Katie's

Mom

By J.J. Stuart

Standard Legal Blurb

"This Collection of Stories is dedicated to beautiful mom's, young and old, who somehow manage to raise kids, work full-time, keep husbands from doing stupid things, and look good while doing it!"

-JJ Stuart

Watching Katie's Mom

In the seaside town of San Altra, nestled against the warm waters of the Pacific, the bright white buildings contrasted with the rich tapestry of the blue ocean. Tourists, mainly dressed in flip-flops and beachwear, flocked to the surrounding beaches and resort hotels, while enjoying cool breezes and white sands. Cars and mopeds added to the hum of music and laughter of people enjoying an easy afternoon. Summer in San Altra always had a carefree atmosphere.

Along one of San Altra's streets, not far from the beach but off the beaten path, stood a small yoga studio. It wasn't fancy or flashy or decorated with advertisements aimed at tourists or filled with loud music. It was a plain two-story building with faded paint, that somehow enhanced the rustic Zen-like atmosphere of the place. The yoga studio was nestled between a coffee shop and a bookstore, with parking in the rear shared by all three businesses. With all the bustle on the streets, with so many flashy signs and overlapping music, one might miss this studio. Many tourists did. Sometimes, though, a person would walk by, cast a quick glance through the open door, and say to themselves, 'Oh they have a yoga studio here,' before continuing on their journey. Though the clientele were mainly locals, sometimes tourists did find their way in, and they were always welcome. The studio had been there for thirty years and didn't advertise. It never had and didn't need to because classes were packed year-round.

In the dimly lit interior of that studio, dressed in black yoga pants and a pink sports bra, was thirty-four-year-old and single-mother, Clara Young. She was doing a strenuous pose along with the rest of the class and paused to brush the disheveled hair from her eyes. Though fit and toned, the pose was too much for Clara. She finally gave up, sat back, and let out a frustrated huff. While regaining her composure and tucking more of her brunette hair back into place, Clara glanced at the people around the class. So many sweaty bodies, she thought. She hated feeling sweaty, but what she hated, even more, was being the only one unable to complete the pose. The air inside the studio was hot despite the large fan standing in the doorway. But San Altra was always like this in the summer.

Looking down, Clara grabbed her water bottle, popped the cap, and took a quick gulp. The water was tepid but felt good going down her dry throat, anyway. Her friend, Jackie, on the next mat over, groaned quietly and broke the same strenuous pose Clara had given up trying. Jackie grimaced and glanced at Clara before grabbing her own water bottle. Clara pasted a smile on her face as she looked at her friend. She hated how Jackie never seemed to perspire. Jackie; the perfect bubbly bouncing blonde with no kids, no husband, and perfect breasts.

"Try it again ladies, you're doing very well," Steve encouraged them from the front of the class. Steve was their yoga instructor and had spied the two women resting when he looked up from his pose.

Steve was handsome Clara thought–for a man in his fifties. But she hadn't always thought so. When Clara first met Steve, she thought him nothing special at all. Just another middle-aged man trying desperately to hold on to his youth hitting on younger women to see if he's still got it. He was polite, and cordial but not the type of man that made your heart go thump. At least not for Clara. Jackie, on the other hand, had a thing for him. This perturbed Clara because she couldn't see what all the fuss was about. He wasn't rich. He wasn't famous. And besides, he had funny hair.

Over time, the more Clara listened to Jackie talk about Steve, the more his odd looks and non-fashion sense grew on her. Maybe he was handsome she thought. He was definitely borderline. But perceptions change. She liked his mop of graying hair. Hair that always appeared muddled and yet stylish at the same time. She couldn't decide if the style was purposeful or accidental. She also noted that he was surprisingly muscled and toned compared to most men his age. At least that was another point in favor of liking him, other than his hair. Another point would have to be his big cock, Clara thought with an amused inner smile. To be honest, the last quality wasn't one she had discovered until recently.

Rolling her large brown eyes, Clara tucked an escaped strand of hair around her ear and glanced at Jackie who was hiding a smirk. Steve never permitted his clients to relent or slack in their efforts to achieve perfection. He liked being dominant and maybe that's why Jackie had a crush on him. It had to be either his dominant personality or his big cock, Clara decided. She knew Jackie's inclination towards well-endowed men, so guessed it had something to do with the latter.

Taking a determined breath, Clara set her jaw and resumed her pose. Her task today was to start in Downward Dog, bending over while keeping her legs straight. Then, with her palms resting on the ground and her bum in the air, she formed an inverted 'V'. She could feel the tension on her calves and hamstrings as her body protested. After a deep breath, she walked her hands inwards, transitioning into the Hands to Feet pose which was basically wrapping your fingers around your ankles and touching your shins with your forehead. She could have done this easily as a teenager, but not now, not as a single mom in her thirties. The frustration of it was only amplified by the heat.

As a single mother, her life had consisted mainly of trying to pay the bills and raise her daughter, Katie. Now that Katie was about to turn nineteen and heading off to college, Clara found she had more time to enjoy the things in life she felt she missed as a young teen mom. Taking up yoga, for example, had been a lifelong dream, though if you asked her at this moment she might tell you otherwise.

Peering over, Clara noticed that Jackie was also settling into Hands to Feet. Not to be bested by her friend, Clara pushed herself harder until she felt the back of her legs straining. Unfortunately, this was where her flexibility ended. To her satisfaction, she noticed that Jackie was also struggling, unaware that her large natural breasts acted as a buffer against her legs. Seeing Jackie struggle against her boobs only made Clara chuckle all the more.

As Clara slowly bounced her torso in an effort touch her forehead to her shins, she peered back through her legs and spotted a greasy looking man in a purple tracksuit behind her. When the man saw her gaze, he quickly dropped his beady eyes and looked away. He was staring at our asses Clara realized with surprise. You just didn't do that in a yoga class– it was one of the unwritten social rules. The disgusting pervert had taken advantage of their compromising positions to enjoy a little peep show! Flustered, Clara was about to warn Jackie when the instructor interrupted her thoughts.

"Ok class, that's it for today," Steve announced as he unfolded from a pose he was holding and glanced at the wall clock. "Well done to everyone. I am seeing progress all around and I hope to see you again next week."

Around the class relieved and thankful people unfolded themselves from various poses and began to get on their feet. Because it was hot, and everyone was sweating, the usually cheery post session banter was a bare minimum.

Clara collapsed in a happy heap, rolling out her tongue and sprawling her arms across the mat as she feigned death. Jackie laughed and sank to her knees, her heavy breasts barely jiggling when she did so. Clara propped herself on an elbow and grabbed her water bottle. She shot a 'busted' look at the perverted man in purple as he made a hasty retreat to the back of the studio. Despite her glare, Clara felt a perverse enjoyment in knowing someone found her body desirable. She just wished it wasn't *that* man. He had looked like a man that would lure kids into windowless vans with candy and she suppressed a creepy shudder. Being noticed only made Clara wish she could find the right man–a handsome man–to take an interest in her. Not that she needed a man, Clara reminded herself. She had come this far in life and raised a child on her own without a man. Still, it would be nice to have someone to share her life with who wasn't a pervert or who didn't have strange hair sticking out in all directions. Just a handsome muscular man to snuggle with who wouldn't mind opening jars or rubbing her shoulders and who wanted to grow old with her. Was that asking too much?

"I wish I was eighteen, this would be so much easier," Jackie said tossing her long blonde hair back and disturbing Clara's thoughts. Jackie's water bottle was empty, and she snapped the lid shut in disgust.

"What are you talking about?" Clara said. She discreetly admired Jackie's shapely legs and heavy firm breasts that many people swore were fake but were not. "You look great."

Jackie snorted. "I'm fat. Poor life choices."

"Well, apparently you still have it, because that pervert dude behind us was totally checking you out," Clara said in thrilled disgust.

"The guy in the seventies purple tracksuit? Girl, he was totally checking you out! I didn't want to say anything, but every time you bent over, his eyes were like laser beams on that little ass of yours." Jackie laughed as she got to her feet and made little laser beam shooting sounds.

"Stop that," Clara said flatly, not believing a word she heard. "Anyhow, let's get going, I really need to set up for Katie's birthday party. You're still coming right?"

Jackie nodded and began rolling up her yoga mat. "So Katie is finally turning nineteen, wow. I can't believe how old we're getting. I'll be at the party for sure. Will there be any college boys attending by chance?"

"Ladies," Steve said, his deep voice interrupting their conversation. He stood a few feet away with arms folded, his mop of hair sticking out every-which-way.

Clara and Jackie quickly turned their heads, hoping he hadn't been listening.

"I do believe that your monthly membership fees are due," he said with a knowing smirk while looking at both of them. "Would you both like to arrange payment? Once everyone has left, of course."

Clara grimaced. Not this again. She had to set up the birthday decorations and didn't have time for a sexual romp. Besides, the whole trading sex for memberships was getting lame. It had been Jackie's idea so she could sleep with Steve. And it worked. Maybe too well.

Jackie grinned and touched Steve's arm. "I wouldn't want us to be delinquent in payment but I haven't told Clara about our arrangement yet. Could you be a sweetheart and give us a few minutes?"

"Of course," Steve said with a bow. He straightened and turned, his gaze lingering on Jackie's ample bust. He strode towards the back of the studio and began collecting mats while talking to the man in the purple tracksuit.

"I don't have time for this right now," Clara said in hushed tones casting a glance towards Steve's backside. "Why can't we just pay like everyone else?"

"Now what fun would there be in that?" Jackie said with a twinkle in her eye.

Clara lowered her voice to a whisper. "What kind of arrangement were you talking about? He better not spunk in my hair like last time. You have any idea how hard it is to get that stuff out?"

"He did make a giant mess," Jackie said remembering it well. "You were so shocked and so cute getting your very first facial. I remember you froze, so startled you couldn't even move while he spurted all over your pretty face. And before you mention it again, I'm still sorry I forgot to tell you beforehand that he shoots a lot. It was incredible to watch though. Now come on, be honest, tell me you didn't cum hard last time too? I mean *really* hard?"

Clara blushed recalling her last encounter with Steve. There was so much cum on her face she couldn't even open her eyes and had to beg Jackie to run and get her a towel. To be fair, though, she did have pretty intense climaxes of her own the last time she was with Steve and Jackie. It was probably because of the newness of the situation, or the strangeness of it. Maybe the idea that she was going to let a man cum all over her face for the first time in her life, had excited her. Was all that really a month ago? The sudden realization that she hadn't gotten lucky since their last 'payment' only made Clara feel depressed. How sad is my life that the only action I get is from a fifty-year-old yoga instructor? Can I go another month? Do I want to?

"I don't want to get messy," Clara stated, feeling her resistance fade. She could use another orgasm or two. "I have to get Katie's party stuff done. What type of mom would I be if her party wasn't ready because mommy was getting laid? So what's this arrangement he was asking about?"

Jackie smiled. "Steve expressed an interest in trying anal with us, and I agreed. This time, when he cums, I'll make sure he doesn't get any on you. I promise."

"Anal? You're such a whore," Clara teased. When Jackie didn't laugh, Clara blinked. "You're serious? You want to try butt sex with that man?"

"If it makes him happy, then yes. You don't have to, but I'm going to let him."

"You're seriously going to let him put his cock in your ass?" Clara asked with wide eyes, her mind still not comprehending what she heard.

The whole 'payment' thing had started as a lark because Jackie found Steve attractive and wanted to concoct a plan to have sex with him. Clara didn't really fancy older men but decided to throw caution to the wind and played along. What she thought was going to be a drab, slightly weird experience, turned out to be the most intense sex of her life. At first, Clara had thought they would have a few 'sessions' with Steve and get free yoga classes but it soon became obvious that Jackie wanted this to be a regular threesome fantasy. What did she see in him? Clara reluctantly decided she would have one more fantasy session with Steve and Jackie, but then that would be it. She didn't need to trade sex for free memberships and neither did Jackie.

"Well, are you game to try it?" Jackie pressed.

"Anal?" Clara shook her head. "Definitely not. You can try butt sex, but I'm not into that, sorry. I'll support you and do other stuff, but no, not in my butt."

"Thank you for being there for me," Jackie said and spun towards Steve.

Clara felt an odd sexual thrill course through her body. She did enjoy the bondage play and Steve, despite his age, was very considerate in satisfying both of their needs. The idea of letting him put his cock in her ass sounded both painful and too intimate. This would definitely be the last session she told herself.

Jackie gestured for Clara to follow her. Together they approached Steve and adopted the submissive role-playing poses he taught them last time. Hands at your sides, head down and eyes on the floor. No talking unless spoken to

"We are ready to serve you, Master," Jackie said quietly, shooting Clara a wink.

Clara remained silent, suppressing a silly grin of her own. She always felt a little nervous and ridiculous at the beginning of their role-playing. Despite both of them being strong independent women, it was important for both Jackie and Clara to stay in character and assume submissive personalities. It was thrilling in a way to pretend to be someone's sex slave–to pretend to be powerless, she thought. Steve enjoyed it, and though he was sometimes strict, he always made sure both of them left feeling very satisfied–and himself of course. Master's needs always come first. At that moment, while playing a submissive slave, Clara realized just how much she needed an orgasm. Had it really been a whole month? If anyone asked, she would deny it.

Steve turned and placed his hands on his hips. He didn't say anything at first, letting the long silence start to work on the two nervous women. He simply looked them over for a moment as if deciding something. Then he slowly walked around Jackie and Clara inspecting their bodies–or deciding how he would use them. Once more standing in front of the two women he tapped a finger against his chin. Neither Jackie nor Clara had moved. Despite this being a fantasy role-playing thing, he was none-the-less impressed with what both women had learned.

"Have you two made a decision about my request?"

Jackie nodded but kept her eyes on the floor. "I am willing to try it, provided Master is gentle, but Clara is not. I could not persuade her, Master."

"Is this true?" Steve turned towards Clara.

"Yes, Master. The Slave is not ready to try that, sorry."

"Master respects your limits and appreciates your honesty," Steve said with a hint of disappointment. "Now, I must lock the front door and close the bay window. While I do that, I want you two slaves to start kissing each other. What are your safe words?"

Jackie at once piped, "Pickles, Sir."

Clara, on the other hand, blinked for a moment as she stared at the floor, her mind still processing the kissing part. Was he for real? He wanted her to start kissing her best friend? She had never kissed Jackie. At least he respected her wishes and wouldn't be putting anything in her butt, but asking her to kiss Jackie seemed to be another line he wanted them to cross. She had never agreed to girl-on-girl action and was uncertain whether to agree or not.

Steve cleared his throat reminding Clara that he was waiting.

"Um, Radishes, Sir," Clara said, her mind racing. Her safe word was radishes. She could feel her cheeks flushing and hated that about herself. Even the slightest embarrassment turned her cheeks red and kissing her best friend in front of another man was most definitely embarrassing.

"Very good," Steve said, not noticing Clara's hesitation. "You may begin."

Taking the lead, Jackie turned and slung her arms around Clara's shoulders drawing her closer. Clara blinked and stared into sultry blue eyes. Jackie leaned closer and their lips touched. Steve was watching with amusement as Clara froze, a startled look on her face, while Jackie started planting soft kisses. The shock was momentary though. Clara giggled and embraced her friend and then softly returned kisses of her own. This was definitely something new, Clara thought. Why had they never kissed before today? Steve was indeed pushing her limits and opening up new experiences for them both. Clearing her thoughts, Clara decided to relax and go with it and was rewarded with a warm sensation in her pussy.

Steve quickly closed the front door and locked the bay window before returning. He stood and watched the two women. It didn't take long for him to rub the bulge that sprouted in his shorts. After a few minutes of watching, he finally cleared his throat once more.

"Yes, Master?" Jackie replied breaking her embrace and peering at the bulge in his shorts.

"I've always enjoyed you two ladies, and today I have something special."

"Oh?" Jackie said. "Do tell us, Master."

Steve smiled and pointed towards his back office which leads upstairs to his private apartment and studio. "Today we will be upstairs. I have new floor mats and air conditioning."

"Not down here today, Master? This should be fun," Jackie said. She embraced Clara and planted another passionate kiss on her lips before taking her hand and heading towards his office.

"Slaves don't walk."

Both Clara and Jackie stopped in their tracks.

"You two will crawl on hands and knees for my enjoyment," Steve ordered while adjusting the bulge in his shorts.

Crawl? Clara thought Steve might be pushing this role playing thing a bit too far. Clara was about to protest until she saw Jackie get down. Is she really going to crawl? Swallowing her pride, Clara got on her hands and knees as well. She hadn't crawled around like this since she was chasing Katie as a toddler and quite frankly she felt a little degraded and silly. She knew Steve would be enjoying the view of their tightly wrapped asses bound in yoga pants. There was no way to hide any of her curves. It was humiliating to crawl on the ground because a man told her to. Maybe that was the point. The humiliation of crawling seemed to stimulate her own arousal. No one would ever treat her like this in real life. Maybe that was the thrill of it.

Clara and Jackie began to crawl with slow awkward movements towards the back of the studio. They passed through a doorway leading to Steve's office and a curtain of hanging privacy beads which jingled and tinkled in their wake. Clara noticed the smell of cooked rice and vegetables and thought of her own hunger briefly before she followed Jackie up the set of stairs leading to the private apartment and studio.

"Up the steps like good little dogs," Steve said.

Clara glanced at Jackie and was about to ask if this was worth free yoga lessons but Jackie was enjoying herself and took to the steps with the vigor of a puppy. Taking a deep breath, Clara followed, though her hands and knees were beginning to feel sore.

Clara was certain Steve would get quite the sensual display of her rump as she mounted the steps. Yoga pants didn't offer a lot of privacy at the best of times, and Clara was sure that wiggling upstairs left nothing to the imagination at all. Was it a surprise that he wanted to try anal with them? The thought of Steve gazing at her ass made her feel dirty and yet aroused.

She could already feel the slippery heat between her legs. Who knew crawling could get you horny? She felt her face flush despite the fact that Steve had already seen her naked quite a few times already. Still, the act of being degraded did thrill her in a perverse sort of way, though she would never admit that openly. She was glad that Jackie was with her. Alone, she would never have the courage to do something like this with a man she barely knew.

The top of the stairs revealed a simple, yet tasteful space. The training area was identical to the one downstairs but equipped with better mats and better lighting. This was where Steve held private lessons for those willing to pay. Half of the upstairs floor was sectioned off by a wall covered in floor to ceiling mirrors. The wall separated the studio from Steve's personal quarters. The wall of mirrors reflected sunlight from the windows giving the smaller space the illusion of being larger than it really was.

The cool air conditioning was a welcome sensation on her skin, and Clara was thankful the crawling was over. Spotting a couch against the wall, she was tempted to crawl over to it, but reminded herself it would be out of character for a submissive slave. Keeping her eyes lowered and head down, she simply remained on her hands and knees beside Jackie and waited for a command. Though somewhat new to the whole bondage lifestyle, she was learning quickly.

"Slaves, you will remove your tops and show Master your titties. Is that understood?" Steve said.

"Yes, Master," both women replied almost in unison.

Jackie took the lead and sat back on her haunches. She grabbed her top and peeled it up and over her head. Her thick heavy breasts flopped out with barely a bounce as she tossed the shirt away.

Clara always felt a little self-conscious of her own breasts whenever Jackie was around. She leaned back and reached around to unclasp her pink sports bra. She pulled the straps off her shoulders and felt her nipples react to the cool air. Though her breasts were smaller than Jackie's, they were still well rounded with upturned nipples. Perky handfuls were how she described them.

Steve had moved to a comfortable chair beside the mirrored wall and after adjusting his cock through his shorts took a seat. He picked up a thin bamboo cane no thicker than a pencil and motioned for the two women to crawl over to him and kneel. As Jackie and Clara crawled topless, their breasts dangled and swayed, pulled down and stretched by their own weight. Steve devoured the sight with his eyes. There were few things he enjoyed more that to watch the swaying dangling breasts of a bent over woman. Clara and Jackie sat back on their knees in front of Steve's chair and resumed submissive poses with heads down and hands resting at their sides. He tapped the pencil-thin cane in his hand and smiled, taking his time to follow the shape and outline of each breast with his eye.

"Master is pleased," Steve said.

He stood and undid his shorts. Both Clara and Jackie kept their eyes lowered, but they knew what he was doing. His shorts dropped and bunched around his ankles. He flicked them aside and started stroking his cock.

"You may look at it," Steve said, letting his erect cock stand on its own.

Jackie and Clara turned their faces upward and fixed their eyes on his impressive manhood. Jackie made a happy humming sound in her throat. Clara eyed his cock with interest but then looked at the bamboo cane in his hand with some suspicion.

"Cup your breasts with your hands and open your mouths. Keep them open. It's time to show gratitude to Master," Steve said, his voice edged with desire.

It was an easy command for both Clara and Jackie to obey. Cupping their breasts and opening their mouths, they waited obediently. Steve left them in that pose while he slowly walked around, his eyes taking in every curve and shape of the topless women kneeling before him. He gently traced the tip of his thin cane across their backsides giving both women shivers of pleasure.

"When I offer you my cock, you will suck it with gratitude for being allowed the privilege. So long as your blowjob amuses me, I will continuously whip the breasts of your friend. Should you falter in your efforts or waiver in your enthusiasm, I will switch mouths and whip your breasts instead. It is therefore in your best interest to keep Master amused."

Clara felt her cheeks flush again. It was humiliating kneeling on the floor waiting for a man to put his cock in your mouth. Seeing her face redden, Steve moved and stood in front of her. She held her mouth open and peered up at him, her large brown eyes pleading. He slipped his cock between her lips, and she closed her mouth around it, tasting his saltiness. The moment Clara began moving her head back and forth, Steve began to tap Jackie's cupped breasts with the cane. They weren't hard taps, but they were numerous and unrelenting.

Jackie groaned and her face contorted in discomfort.

"Keep your mouth open," Steve ordered. Jackie quickly obeyed after one particularly sharp strike.

The sound of Jackie's heavy breasts being flicked and whacked over and over was strangely motivating for Clara. She didn't want her breasts whipped, so she put extra effort into keeping her mouth working on his cock.

"This one is giving me great pleasure. I might keep my cock in her mouth for a while. She is way more skilled than you, Slave Jackie."

Despite her efforts to suck his large cock, Clara giggled. That was enough of a falter for Steve. She felt his cock withdrawn from her startled mouth. Blinking, Clara peered up and saw Steve step sideways, his cock glistening with her saliva. Jackie's eager mouth was open, and she willingly took him. A moment later Clara winced as the bamboo cane began to strike her bare breasts over and over. *Why did I giggle? Ouch!*

Clara kept her mouth open as instructed and started writhing under the relentless taps on her breasts. That was the point, and it amused Steve to watch. She wiggled and groaned and begged in the most humiliating and demeaning way for Steve to let her suck him again. Jackie, though, was having none of it and worked his shaft with eagerness and an expertise that Clara didn't have.

Eventually, Steve pulled his cock from Jackie's mouth. "Look how eager she is to suck me off," he said and stepped back to Clara.

Clara forced her mouth around his cock and eagerly started to suck, glad that the relentless caning was over. Her breasts were tender now. Jackie whimpered as her boobs now became the focus of his cane.

"You see, all a slave needs is a little motivation. Now I'm finally getting a quality blowjob. Should I cum in your mouth, Clara? Would you like that?"

Clara wasn't wild about the idea considering how much he ejaculated on her face the last time. In her aroused state she continued to suck and eagerly nodded. If he wanted to cum in her mouth, then she would let him.

"I might, but then again I might not. My cock is starting to tingle. I think we'll stop for now and move on. Well done my little whores," Steve said. He withdrew his cock from Clara's mouth and wiped it on her flushed cheeks like her face was nothing more than a washcloth. Clara felt like a dirty whore. No man had ever used her face to clean his cock with and she savored the way it made her even hornier.

When Steve stepped back, both Clara and Jackie were breathing hard and had saliva and drool hanging off their chins. Neither closed their mouths or stopped cupping their now tender breasts. Part of being submissive was waiting for Master to give the commands.

Steve rested on the chair and gazed at the two women kneeling on the floor and mused. He enjoyed the sight of them, and their willingness to be submissive. He would have blown his load already if he hadn't wanted to stay hard and try anal with Jackie. Too bad Clara was reluctant, he thought. He would dearly love to sink his cock into her tight little behind, but he respected her wishes. In time, though, she might change her mind. That would be a day to remember, Steve thought.

"Slave Jackie, you may stand and come here," Steve said.

Jackie obeyed and got to her feet. Her heavy breasts were red from the caning but nothing that wouldn't soon fade. She carefully walked over and stood in front of Steve, her head lowered and eyes on the floor.

"Yes, Master?"

"There is a bottle of lubricant over on that table," he paused and pointed to the bottle. "I want you to begin preparing your anus for penetration."

Jackie nodded and obediently retrieved the bottle. Next, Steve focused on Clara who was still kneeling with her mouth open and breasts cupped. He liked Clara, she was more reserved, but her orgasms were more intense.

"Slave Clara, you may sit on my lap and ride my cock."

Clara blushed deeper. "Yes, Master," she said quietly liking his crude talk.

"Ask first," Steve added when she started to move.

Clara froze and admonished herself. Her face burned with humiliation and desire. "Please, Master may I ride your cock?"

"Beg for it."

Clara struggled to keep her eyes lowered, but nodded. "Please, Sir. I desperately want your cock inside of me. I'm begging you to let me ride it."

"You may mount my cock, but remember this is for my pleasure and not yours. You may not cum without permission."

Steve watched as Clara came closer. She was blushing, and he loved that about her. She was a gorgeous woman, and he doubted she would ever consider a relationship with him. He sighed. No matter, at least he was about to fuck her.

Clara straddled him in the chair, careful not to press her knees into him then reached for his hard cock and lowered herself onto it. The tip found her warm folds, and she wiggled the head until it found her opening. Once the tip was inside, she placed her hands on his shoulders and began to work him in, her bare breasts only inches from his hungry eyes.

"That's it, you feel so tight, slave," Steve said. She was a lot tighter than Jackie, he noticed with satisfaction. Probably because she got a lot less sex. Whatever the case, though, Clara's tight cunt felt like a warm glove around his shaft.

Clara closed her eyes and let the thickness of his cock fill her. She didn't really want to gaze into his eyes and be reminded she was riding a fifty-year-old man. If she squeezed her eyes shut, she could imagine she was riding a young muscular man. Images of her daughter's boyfriend, Jacob, filled her mind. He was handsome. She rode Steve's cock thinking about Jacob. She clenched her thigh muscles and let her own wetness lubricate his cock until she fully impaled herself on it. Clenching her teeth and grimacing with pleasure, Clara proceeded to lift herself up and then let her weight drop her back down. Waves of pleasure cascaded through her. She hadn't had sex in a month and her body was responding by jumping into overdrive. Steve grabbed her breasts and fondled them as she rose and fell quicker, her face a mask of pleasure. Quicker and quicker she humped his delicious cock feeling her orgasm build and build. She was nearly there. She dug her nails into his shoulder and began grinding herself on his cock, her breathing becoming quick gasps of pleasure. She felt her orgasm coming and began to pant. Just a little more.

"That's enough," Steve ordered and grabbed her wrists, forcing her to stop in mid-stride.

Clara's eyes flew open, and her face contorted in sexual frustration. *What? Why did he make me stop?*

"Did Master give you permission to cum?"

Clara bit her lip in frustration, her eyes pleading. "Please, Master, may I cum?"

"No, you may not. Off you get," he said patting her bare ass. Putting his hands under her arms he lifted her small frame off him with ease. For a man in his fifties, he was strong. He pointed to a spot on the floor and ordered her to kneel and wait.

Clara groaned, her orgasm was receding and her wet pussy ached to be satisfied. Had he really ordered her to kneel and wait? She wanted to cum, but part of the role-playing was learning to be submissive. He would let her cum, but not until he wanted her too. Clara forced herself to remain obedient as she tried to slow her breathing and her racing heart. She nodded, and knelt, folding her hands in her lap. She couldn't remember being so horny. Steve took a perverse pleasure it seemed in denying her orgasms.

"You will not touch yourself, and you will not cum until I decide," Steve said.

"Yes, Master," Clara replied, trying to hide the frustration on her face.

"You nearly made me cum, Slave Clara. That would have been bad. Master has another Slave to give him pleasure. You can wait."

Despite the crude remark, Clara's face brightened. Had she nearly made him cum? It was a compliment of sorts. She could have made him cum. He wanted to cum, but he wanted to try anal with Jackie even more. She smiled to herself.

"Thank you, Master," Clara said.

Steve patted her on the head. "I want you to kneel close-by and watch Jackie taking it up the ass. Because you were so obedient, you may masturbate and cum while watching me fuck Jackie."

Normally Clara would find such language vulgar but in the safe realm of role-playing, she was able to embrace the thrill that coursed through her body as she nodded and offered thanks to him. She was actually quite curious to watch.

"Are you ready for Master's cock?" Steve asked Jackie. She had been lubricating herself while watching Clara ride him with wide hungry eyes. Now those hungry eyes rested on his erect cock.

Jackie nodded.

Turning to Clara, Steve asked, "What position should I have her in?"

Startled that he would even ask her, or that she would have the faintest idea what a good anal sex position was, Clara could only blink for a moment.

"I... I'm not sure, Master," Clara said.

"If I was to fuck you in the ass, how would you want to be positioned?"

Clara flushed. She had never heard a man talk that way before; it was so crude and vulgar and animalistic and she loved it. She thought for a moment having never considered such a position. "I suppose on my knees, Master, with my butt in the air? Perhaps my face on the floor?"

"Wouldn't you want to watch your first anal experience?" Steve asked.

Clara crinkled her nose and considered his words, feeling slutty for even answering with a nod. "I suppose so, Master. Why not ask her what position she would like?"

"Because she doesn't get a say in the matter. I am asking you because I am curious what you would choose," Steve explained. He turned towards Jackie. "You will lay on your back and pull your knees up and to the sides."

Jackie nervously moved onto her back and grabbed her knees and spread them wide. Her blue eyes darted towards Steve's large cock and she seemed to be on the verge of changing her mind. Clara wouldn't hold it against her friend for backing out. She wouldn't want such a thick cock forced up her ass either.

"If this is too much, you may use your safe word and I will stop," Steve said. He noticed her nervousness too. Clara held her breath.

"No, Master," Jackie said tightening down her courage. "This is something, Slave has always wanted to try. Slave trusts Master to be gentle. I want to do this, Sir. As a gift to you."

Steve seemed moved and knelt on the floor, positioning himself between her legs. He then leaned forward and placed his knuckles on the floor on either side of Jackie and lowered his face to hers and gently kissed her on the lips. Jackie responded nervously at first, but as they continued to kiss, she relaxed more. His gentle kisses had melted the last of her reservations. When he finished, he leaned back and Jackie was smiling at him. She pulled her knees apart wider as a signal she was ready.

Steve looked up. "Clara?"

"Yes, Master?" Clara said snapping out of her private thoughts.

"Master would like you to straddle her face and hold her legs apart while she eats your pussy."

Clara blinked in shock.

Steve chuckled and pointed towards Jackie's head. "Straddle her face while you hold her legs for her. Unless you would like to use your safe word right now?"

There was a hint of disappointment in his eyes. Clara knew this was a big step for her. She had never kissed Jackie before today and now he was asking her rub her pussy in her friend's face? She hesitated while Steve patiently waited for her to comply.

"Jackie?" Clara asked, breaking the no talking rule, but Steve didn't mind.

"It's okay. I've wanted to do that to you for years," Jackie breathed.

Feeling stunned, Clara blinked in disbelief. Had Jackie wanted to lick her pussy for years, and she never knew? Clara never even suspected that Jackie had a lesbian bone in her body. The realization made Clara feel uneasy. This was a lot absorb, and she was already pushing her comfort levels. Steve started stroking his cock as he waited, unaware of her thoughts.

"Do you like being licked by your best friend?" Steve asked, his cock heavy with lust as he slowly stroked it.

Clara shook her head. "Radishes."

Not expecting Clara to use her safe word, Steve's eyebrows shot up and his mouth opened in surprise. His shock was short-lived, though, and he nodded. The safe word must be respected.

"Too far for you Clara?" Steve asked, breaking character.

"Sort of, yes," Clara replied. "I never kissed a girl before today and asking me to straddle her face for oral is just a bit too far for me just now. Sorry."

Steve held up his hand. "No apologies needed. You reached your limit, and that's fine. We can stop, or would you like to continue?"

Feeling relieved, Clara leaned forward and planted a kiss on Steve's cheek, whispering her thanks into his ear. He seemed surprised but nodded. Leaning back, Clara took hold of Jackie's legs while straddling her face. She peered down at her friend who was nervously looking up.

"I feel comfortable like this, just no oral, Jackie. I'm sorry, please don't be mad at me, but I'm just not ready for that. Okay?"

Jackie giggled. "It's perfectly fine, I still have a perfect view from down here."

"Oh stop it!" Clara laughed.

Steve seemed relieved too. A new idea came to him. "Would you feel comfortable masturbating while straddling her face so she can watch?"

"I can definitely do that," Clara said with a slight blush. She looked down at her friend's upturned face. "As long as you don't mind."

"Oh I don't mind at all, babe," Jackie said with enthusiasm.

Steve grinned.

"Can I begin, Master?" Clara asked, slipping back into the role playing game.

"You may," Steve answered, glad that Clara was still up for more. He looked at the wet prize between Jackie's legs and then up as Clara began to masturbate. The sight of the gorgeous brunette masturbating made his cock throb with desire. Gently wiggling the tip of his cock against Jackie's wet pussy lips, he paused, his cock parting her folds. As Clara closed her eyes, he drank in the sight of her beautiful face bathed in pleasure and then forcefully sank his cock into Jackie in one steady motion. Jackie wasn't tight, and the feeling was a little disappointing, but Steve didn't say anything. Once buried to the hilt, he held still. Jackie was soaking wet and more than ready, but he wanted to enjoy the sight of Clara. He slowly withdrew and easily in again. After a pause he withdrew and thrust harder, and then harder still, slowly building up a steady rhythm and pace, never once taking his eyes off Clara's face.

Though he would never say this openly, as far as he was concerned, Jackie was just a warm place to drain his balls. Yeah, she had great tits and a cute face, but his real desire was for Clara. It always had been, from the moment he first laid eyes on her. She was masturbating for him right now, her large brown eyes squeezed shut and her cute button nose crinkled as she panted and groaned. He started delivering harder thrusts, slamming his cock into Jackie while he eagerly anticipated Clara's climax and imagining it was his cock giving her pleasure.

He liked Jackie as a person, he thought. But if it wasn't for Clara masturbating only a few feet away, he probably would have gone soft already. In his mind, Jackie was just a well-used stepping stone to get closer to Clara. He had hoped when he suggested anal to Jackie that she would have convinced Clara. As he continued to slam his cock in and out of Jackie he wasn't surprised that the idea of anal was too much for Clara. In his mind, Clara was much more reserved and had more self-respect. In his mind, most women given the choice will pass on butt-sex.. Clara held Jackie's one legs by her ankle, while using her other hand to stimulate her clit. Jackie's other leg was held by Steve who used it for leverage as he fucked. With every thrust of Steve's cock, Clara's breasts jiggled and her probing fingers brought her aroused pussy closer to orgasm. Clara opened one eye and peered down at Steve's cock, fascinated and excited by the sight of it pounding her friend's pussy over and over. She had never watched another woman being fucked up close.

Steve slowed his thrusts and finally came to a stop, his cock still buried in Jackie. He winked at Clara which made her giggle. "Well that was fun," Steve began as he withdrew his wet cock, "How about we try another place?"

Jackie tensed and Clara's eyes went wide with curiosity, her delicate fingers stimulating her clit slowing. This was it, she was going to see anal sex for the first time in her life. Her pussy tingled as she thought about it. Clara watched as he grabbed the bottle of lubricant and flipped the top open. He poured some into his palm and rubbed it over his cock. Clara started rubbing herself harder. Then he squeezed some lubricant between Jackie's legs and started to rub it around, his fingers slipping in and out of her tight butt hole. Jackie groaned quietly.

"Oh!" Clara gasped, causing Steve to look up.

"Do you like watching this?"

Clara's cheeks became red and her breathing quickened. Oh god! Her hand moved faster over her clit. The sensations from her fingers and the idea that Jackie was going to be fucked in the ass threatened to push Clara over the edge.

"Permission to cum, Master!"

Steve shook his head. "Not until Master has cummed. You will not have an orgasm before Master does."

Biting her lip, Clara squeezed her eyes shut and groaned in agony as she tried to ignore the waves of pleasure rising through her body. She nodded, focusing with concentration on her breathing and tried to stop her probing fingers on her clit, but couldn't. She removed her hand, not trusting herself to speak, and tried to comply with Steve's command. It took every ounce of willpower to once again deny herself an orgasm.

His voice throaty, Steve said, "I want you to watch my cock in her ass."

Clara opened one eye and then two. She clenched her jaw and felt her thighs begin to tremble as she obeyed his request. Steve gently pushed Jackie's legs forward until they were wide and her ass tilted upward a little.

"Hold them there," Steve told Clara.

Clara was almost panting with desire when she grabbed Jackie's legs and held them firmly. Steve pressed the tip of his cock against Jackie's tight hole. At first, nothing happened, but then the lubricant began to work and the head of his cock slowly disappeared inside Jackie's anus. From between her thighs, Clara heard a cry from Jackie then a series of hot pants and a high pitched muffled squeal as the cock penetrated her. Steve worked the head back and forth and then pushed deeper in, stretching her tight hole and sinking deeper. Jackie was panting, her hot breath hitting Clara's overstimulated pussy. Her nails dug into Clara's hips. It was too much and Clara in a moment of impulse spread her knees apart and planted her pussy on Jackie's face. Jackie seemed startled but responded with hungry lapping while Clara lost herself grinding her wet clit back and forth.

"Oh god, sorry Master... sorry!" Clara gasped and then shuddered as her own orgasm rippled through her body. She grunted and gyrated her hips as Jackie furiously licked and sucked her clit.

Steve didn't seem to mind that Clara had cummed as he began to quicken his tempo with a series of purposeful thrusts into Jackie's ass. He barely sank his cock all the way in and out a-half-dozen-times before he too grunted, grabbed Jackie's thighs and started pumping her full of cum. Clara was still coming down off her own climax and watched through hazy eyes as his face contorted in pleasure while his balls drained.

Clara was still panting when Steve stopped and opened his eyes. They stared at each other briefly before they both broke into nervous grins.

"That was intense," Clara said. She rolled to the side, revealing a wet mess all over Jackie's face.

"Indeed, it was," Steve agreed, his spent cock still buried in Jackie's ass. "How was it for you my dear?"

Jackie could only giggle as she carefully propped herself up on her elbows. "I think I had like five orgasms. Is my face all messy Steve?"

"Yes, it is," Steve said, brushing some of Jackie's matted blonde hair with his fingers and tucking it behind her ears.

"Um, Steve? Can you take your cock out of my ass now?" Jackie asked wincing in pain and half laughing.

Steve pulled out, his spent cock still half erect and leaving a gaping hole. A trail of cum seeped out and pooled on the floor.

"So you both enjoyed that?" Steve asked. He casually wiped his cock clean on Jackie's inner thigh, before standing up.

Clara was still horny, but it was obvious the role-playing was over now. She brushed some hair from her own sweaty face and nodded. She enjoyed that a lot. A contented sigh escaped her lips. "I think Jackie got the worst of it, though."

"I liked it, but I have to admit that was my first anal experience and it hurt but not too badly, it was like a mix between pain and pleasure. Very arousing. Thank you for cumming on my face, Clara. I enjoyed that."

Clara blushed and held her hand to her mouth. "I'm sorry. I really am. I know I said my safe word, but I just had to cum, and I was holding your ankles. I don't know what came over me."

"Well I know what came all over me," Jackie said and then laughed.

"You broke a command not to cum, but all is forgiven. So long as we all have fun that's what matters. Thank you both. It was a very intense experience. A lot of sexual energy. Consider your yoga fees covered... for another month."

Jackie smiled, but Clara shook her head. "Don't be ridiculous. Of course, we'll pay. This will be my last playtime with you two. It was fun, but I think that was enough boundary pushing for me."

Jackie pouted.

"Well, you are always welcome to join us," Steve said. He was crestfallen.

Clara frowned and looked at them both. "You speak as if there will be more of this between you two. Jackie?"

Jackie hid a guilty smile. "I haven't decided. I do like his cock."

"You are such a whore!" Clara said in jest. "Well, whatever happens, I wish you two the best and thanks for including me, but seriously, I think that was it for me."

"I respect your decision," Steve said as he stood and offered her a hand. Clara took it, and then they both helped Jackie to her feet.

"I need a washroom," Jackie said cupping a hand between her legs to catch the cum leaking out and down her thighs, "Now!"

"We both do," Clara agreed while turning to look at Steve.

He pointed to a small door. "Help yourself. Shower if you want, there are fresh towels if you need them too."

"No showers. I really need to get going. It's my daughter's nineteenth birthday," Clara said. When Steve raised an eyebrow questioningly she added, "I was a teen mom. Had Katie when I was fifteen. Stupid teenager stuff. I got pregnant my first time."

"I see," Steve said. "I'm sure you raised your daughter well."

"I tried," Clara said, suddenly feeling self-conscious. "Guess all this is just me reliving my youth. Thank you though."

"Anytime," Steve said with a chuckle. He watched as Clara followed Jackie into the washroom, enjoying the sight of her naked backside for the last time. He found it curious that despite all the sex they just shared that the two women closed the bathroom door behind them. For privacy?

Moments later the door leading to his bedroom opened and a man's head peered out cautiously. Steve only knew him as Earl, and he was wearing a purple tracksuit. Steve placed his finger to his lips and hushed the man while waving him over with his other hand. The man stepped through and closed the door quietly behind him. His face and beady eyes asked if it was safe but then nodded in understanding when Steve pointed to the closed bathroom door.

"Did you enjoy the show?" Steve asked glancing towards the two-way mirror that gave his beady-eyed friend a complete view of the studio from the privacy of his bedroom. No one knew the wall was a giant two-way mirror.

"I got my rocks off pretty damn hard," Earl said in hushed tones.

"So it's a deal?" Steve asked, trying to delete the image of the man before him having an orgasm. It wasn't something he wanted to picture again. He silently hoped that the man hadn't made a mess.

"You start some naked yoga classes for women, and I will find a buyer for everything we can film. Of course, there will be editing, but this stuff is huge over in Asia," Earl said.

"I'm very happy," Steve said offering Earl a hand but then thinking better of it.

Earl was a sleazy man, Steve thought. Best not shake his hand after the man jerked off to their little sex show. "You should get going. We'll talk money later. Glad you enjoyed it."

"Who was that brunette? She is super hot," Earl asked but Steve was already ushering him towards the stairs leading down.

"Not now. We'll talk later, hurry up and go!" Steve hissed.

Earl nodded and slinked down the stairs. When Steve was certain the man was gone, he turned and retrieved his shorts and the bottle of lubricant. By the time the two women emerged from the washroom, he was flipping through a magazine and smiling to himself.

A short time later, the two women casually walked out of the yoga club and into the bright sunshine of San Altra. Clara enjoyed the light ocean breeze as it cooled her skin. She needed a shower desperately as the sweat of their session had drenched her, despite the air conditioning. Together with Jackie, Clara walked around the building to the private parking lot.

"Coffee and a muffin?" Jackie asked. Her blonde hair was disheveled and her makeup needed retouching, but her bright blue eyes sparkled with clarity.

"Nope, not today," Clara said shaking her head. "I gotta get those birthday decorations up. Besides, you and I both need to go home and shower. I never handled the heat very well, and I'm not getting caught dead sitting in a coffee shop and smelling like a cheap whore."

"I might pop in for a bite. I'll be over at what, seven?"

"Seven is fine. Don't go get a coffee. Just go home, Jackie. Also, nothing expensive for Katie this year. Promise me. That girl is too spoiled as it is."

Grinning, Jackie nodded. "I'm still going for a coffee."

"Fine, ok go. Go before I lose my willpower," Clara said with a wave of her car keys.

"I wouldn't mind seeing if Pedro 'The Love Machine' is working today," Jackie said with a wink and a sigh.

Not after yoga and hot sex Clara thought, but Jackie didn't need to know that.

Pedro was a handsome college boy that both Jackie and Clara found quite pleasing on the eyes. They had secretly named him the 'Love Machine' because his usual attire consisted of flowery Hawaiian shirts and cargo shorts that reminded them of the old 'Love Boat' series on television. It was stupid, but it stuck.

In Clara's fantasy, Pedro was her personal oil boy. She didn't want to know what he was in Jackie's dreams.

"Well, you go home and be a good mom, I'm going to see my Love Machine. Catch you at seven then," Jackie said as she bounced down the street towards the cafe.

Bouncing blondes with bouncing boobs, Clara thought. Pedro was in for a treat. Clara smirked as she got into her sporty convertible. She might have an imaginary visit from Pedro later on in the shower, in the privacy of her own home. She was still horny and having just one orgasm wasn't enough. Nothing wrong with a little reward for a hard yoga class she reasoned while slipping on her sunglasses. Backing out of the parking spot and hitting the throttle, Clara's mind was already churning. Suddenly she was quite eager to get herself home.

About twenty minutes north of San Altra, Clara pulled into her driveway. She was singing along to a silly pop song on the radio about kissing a girl and enjoying the wind in her hair. Her house was large, way too large for her and her daughter, but Clara used a few rooms upstairs for her interior decorating business, so the house space wasn't entirely wasted. Plus there were the tax write-offs. ·

She bought the house because it was outside of San Altra yet still had a nice view of the ocean. At night it was quiet, and the busy sounds of tourists and traffic were seldom heard after eight o'clock. Her driveway was lined with thick shrubs neatly trimmed and manicured. The white concrete driveway was spotless and dotted with palm trees along the edges offering shade. The house itself was two stories and had beautiful wood trim and white stucco walls in the Old Spanish style. All the vegetation, trees and flower gardens around the house not only offered natural privacy but also kept the house cool in the summer months.

Clara unlocked the front door and stepped inside. She was greeted with a cool rush of air that was always refreshing. She closed the heavy wooden door with a resounding thud and locked it. Tossing her keys and sunglasses onto a marble table she looked at herself in the mirror. Wincing, she quickly brushed her windblown hair with her fingers. She didn't have to worry how she looked, not now, but it was just a habit.

No one was home. Katie was still at work and wouldn't be home until after eight. There was plenty of time to prepare Katie's surprise birthday party. First, though, she needed a long, long warm shower and thoughts of Pedro.

Kicking off her shoes, Clara savored the coolness of the marble floors on her bare feet. She slowly padded up the elegant marble spiral staircase to her master bedroom humming remnants of that pop song she heard in the car.

Her master bedroom was her retreat. It had a large king sized four post bed, lots of antique dressers and drawers and art hung neatly along the walls. A large bay window led to a private balcony facing the ocean which filled her room with scents from the gardens during the day and cool ocean breezes at night.

She tossed her gym bag and the yoga mat on the bed and then peeled off her pink sports bra. It felt good to let her breasts out. The red marks from the bamboo cane were fading already. In a few hours, they would be blemish-free again. She tossed her top into the hamper and then slipped off her yoga pants and thong panties and tossed them in as well. Naked and feeling free, Clara headed to her large bathroom and started the shower.

Oh shit, she thought, I forgot pink Pedro. With a naughty grin, she darted naked back into her bedroom. Opening her dresser, and lifting a stack of neatly folded shirts, she found what she was looking for: a bright pink vibrating dildo. It was her favorite among many she had secretly squirreled away. She only used the pink one when thinking about Pedro; imagining it was him. No one knew this little secret - not even her best friend Jackie. Pink vibrating Pedro was her dirty little dildo secret.

Rushing back to the shower, Clara opened the glass door and stepped inside. She loved her marble shower and its size. It was literally large enough for five people and even boasted a tiled bench along one wall. You could sit on that bench and shave your legs or lean back and let the warm water and thoughts of a naughty Pedro fill your body with lust. Today she just wanted some alone time.

* * *

Jacob's eyes flew opened when he heard the heavy front door close with a resounding and unmistakable thump. Katie's mom was home. He rolled over, stretching out on Katie's bed and peered at his girlfriend's alarm clock. He had been napping for a while. He yawned and stared up at the pink ceiling, ignoring the posters of boy bands and the shelving lined with stuffed animals. It was definitely a girl's room.

He had arrived shortly after Clara had left for yoga. After knocking on the door and peering into the garage, he realized no one was home. Because he had Katie's spare key, he unlocked the door and let himself in.

He had originally planned on setting up a birthday surprise in Katie's bedroom but decided after seeing her soft bed, to take a nap instead. He knew she was at work until sometime after supper. He wasn't sure when her shift ended, and now as he lay staring at her pink ceiling he wondered why he was in her room at all. I should have just gone home, he thought.

He could hear Katie's mom and was about to shout out a greeting when he suddenly thought better of it. She might ask what he was doing in her house by himself. He didn't have permission to walk into their home anytime he felt like. Did Clara even know he had a key? He remained silent and listened, more out of caution and indecision than guilt. He waited for her to walk in, ready to offer an excuse, but Clara had gone to her own room it seemed. Jacob could hear her humming a song in the hallway. She's probably just changing, Jacob thought. He'd wait till she came out to say hello, then head probably head home.

He had a thing for Katie's mom. Most men did actually. Sure she was thirty-four, and he was only twenty, but she was a young thirty-four, and still very hot. Jacob found his hand wandering into his shorts. Being in Katie's bedroom without permission and knowing her mom was probably naked in the next room felt both thrilling and bad. It gave him an erection. He smiled at the thought of Clara being naked and stroked himself a little harder.

His ears perked when he heard Clara's private shower come on. She was probably stripping right now, his mind reasoned. He fantasized about her changing and felt a rush of excitement when he imagined "accidentally" walking in on her. She would cover up of course, but he would get enough of a view for his mind to enjoy later.

Jacob sat up hesitating only a moment before jumping to his feet and walking quietly to Katie's bedroom door. He pulled the door back just slightly and peered into the hallway. Clara's bedroom was across the foyer. He found his cock was getting quite excited just thinking she might already be naked. He pulled Katie's door open further and stepped out.

Walking softly he headed across the foyer but caught a glimpse of Clara's backside and quickly darted back. That was close! She hadn't spotted him it seemed. Cautiously he leaned forward until her backside slowly came into view. She was completely nude and standing at her dresser, obviously looking for something. Probably just something to put on after her shower he mused. Like pink panties.

This was so incredibly risky! If she simply looked up at the mirror or looked out into the foyer he would be caught. The thrill aroused him even more. His cock twitched with yearning as his eyes eagerly drank in her shapely legs, and perfect round ass. Who knew Katie's mom had a hot body? He couldn't see her breasts which were disappointing, with her back to him as it was, but the sight of her ass cheeks was more than compensation. He wanted so badly to jerk off now. Part of him wanted to stand in full view of her doorway and defiantly jerk off right there all over her floor. He debated pulling it out in the safety of the hallway, but if she turned and saw him holding his cock. Well, it would be more than awkward, to say the least.

When she turned, Jacob pulled his head back. He half expected her march out into the hallway and confront him, but luck was on his side. She hadn't spotted him. She never even looked up.

He waited to the count of ten, letting his heart slow a little, and then peeked again. She was gone. He cautiously peered further and reasoned she was back in her bathroom. He approached her bedroom, his eyes sweeping the room until they finally rested on a pair of black panties hanging on the edge of the laundry bin. Those were her panties. She must have just been wearing them. Feeling bold, Jacob slipped into the room and scooped them up. He sniffed them and smiled. They were warm and moist.

Already having come this far, and risked so much, he wanted the thrill to continue. He was aroused and curious now. So he decided to peek into the bathroom. Katie's mom had left the door open. Of course, she did. She thought she was alone after all, so there was no need to shut a bathroom door. He could hear the water running and her voice humming a song about kissing a girl. It was going to be his lucky day.

Peering through the small gap between the door hinges Jacob could see Clara. She was standing under the water, her back to him once again. Jacob silently blessed whoever installed the clear glass shower enclosure. With her back still towards him, Jacob carefully adjusted the bathroom door, widening the gap slightly, but not too much. If he stood in the open doorway or stuck his head around the door itself, she would surely spot him. Peering through the gap between the door and the wall was brilliant. Now if she turned, she wouldn't spot him unless she focused on the tiny sliver of space he peered through. It was the perfect cover and all he needed.

Pulling down his shorts and boxers, Jacob eagerly gripped his cock and began to stroke it while his eyes feasted on Clara's backside. He held her black panties in his left hand, ready to use them since there was no tissue handy. Just the thought of blowing his load into her panties excited him. As he stroked, he was careful not to bump the door or make any sounds. This type of operation required skill and finesse.

Clara washed and rinsed her hair. She then turned and lathered her body with soap. Jacob nearly blew his load at the sight of her bare breasts all lathered and wet. Despite how many times he imagined her tits, seeing them for the first time was incredible and intoxicating. He stopped jerking off–just a pause to calm himself. He didn't want to blow his load too soon. This was a show that he might never get again and he wanted to savor every moment. If she looked like she was getting out, he could quickly polish himself off and be out of her room, but so long as she was in the shower naked and wet, he wanted to make this the best jerking off session ever.

After she rinsed herself off, Jacob was certain his secret show was about to come to an end. A few quickened strokes, and he'd be finished. He became curious when instead of getting out; she bent over and picked up a pink object he hadn't noticed before. It took a moment but then he nearly cursed in amazement when he realized she had a sex toy.

Oh my god, Katie's mom uses sex toys?

He stopped jerking and stared through the crack in the door frame, afraid to even blink. Clara tilted the showerhead then sat down on the tile bench letting the warm water wash over her. She then lifted one leg and rested it to the side, spreading herself wide open. She picked up the pink sex toy and Jacob could feel himself willing her to use it.

Oh my fucking god!

She ran the fingers of one hand around her clit before bringing the pink vibrating dildo close with the other hand. She gently massaged the vibrator back and forth, moving it around in small circles before slipping it inside her pussy. She leaned back, closed her eyes and rested her head against the wall in ecstasy. Warm water fell on her glistening body, caressing her skin, kissing it in thousands of places at once. A smile crossed her lips, and she began to masturbate.

Jacob was stunned. He had never seen a woman pleasure herself other than in porn movies accompanied by corny music, and he doubted those women were even really doing it.

This was as real as it gets. A woman in the privacy of her own shower. He had never watched a real woman pleasure herself like this and he had a front row seat!

Fascinated, Jacob slowly rubbed his cock again; his eyes never leaving her body. It didn't take Clara long to have her first little shudder and let out a groan that even he could hear over the water. She increased her tempo, slipping the toy in and out of herself with one hand while the other crept up and massaged her breasts or moved back down and circled her clit. She kept her eyes closed, but her head turned from side to side and her hips bucked ever so slightly, grinding and moving obviously imagining something in her mind.

He began to jerk off harder now, imagining he was in the shower with her. Imagining it was his cock slipping in and out of her. Jacob had the urge to walk into her shower and fuck her right there, but he knew that would be a mistake. She would probably kill him. One thing Jacob knew was that women don't take kindly to being spied on while they pleasure themselves. It's not likely something they would forgive, or forget.

Clara began to pant and groan. Jacob stroked harder, matching his hand stroke to hers, so each time she slipped the toy in, he imagined it was his cock. She shuddered and held the toy against her clit as she brought her legs together and squeezed.

She was having an orgasm!

"Oh, Pedro!" Clara cried out. "Yes! Yes! Oh yes, right there Pedro!"

He watched in amazement as Clara continued her orgasm, drawing it out expertly with soft swirls over her clit. Her breathing turned to panting as both her legs twitched and her toes stretched outward. Then her lips quivered, and she cried out. Jacob felt tense. When her brow creased and her face contorted in orgasm, Jacob felt a twinge in his balls. When she reached up and grabbed her own breast, squeezing and mashing it in her hands, it was too much.

Unable to hold it anymore, Jacob's cock erupted in a violent torrent. He tensed and clamped his mouth shut somehow dropping the black panties. Shit! It was too late. He shot thick gobs of hot cum all over the doorframe and wall. He squeezed his eyes shut and jerked off furiously as powerful contractions fired squirts everywhere. And then it was done.

Holy shit!!!

It was a powerful and violent orgasm. The most intense he ever had, and he momentarily saw stars in his vision. He didn't even know you could cum that hard, and it left him feeling drained. He squeezed the last drops onto the floor and frowned at the mess. Shit! If he didn't clean up fast he was going to get caught, but if he moved too soon and passed out, he would get caught. He quickly peered up to gauge how much time he had.

Clara was standing once again, now lathering and washing clean. He guessed she was done playing with herself too. Perfect timing, he thought. Taking one last mental picture of Clara's naked beauty, Jacob focused on the task at hand. He grabbed Clara's used panties and then cleaned the mess he made as best he could. With most of it gone, he backed out of

Clara's room and retreated into Katie's room where he flopped onto her bed. He knew he missed some spots but there was nothing he could do about that. He carefully held Clara's ruined panties by the very corner and shook his head in dismay. They were soaked with globs of his sticky semen and ruined beyond repair. He cringed and then sat upright and leaned over the side of the bed and tossed them into Katie's waste basket.

Laughing at the dangerous thrill of watching Katie's mom, Jacob fell backward on the bed, his head sinking into Katie's pink pillow. He grinned and ran a hand through his hair. It was his best jerk off session ever and he couldn't believe how hard he had cum.

He closed his eyes and took a deep satisfying breath. He could hear Clara a few minutes later singing to herself. He thought she must be toweling off and getting dressed. Jacob tucked his arms behind his head but kept his eyes closed as he listened to her voice. He hoped he didn't hear any sudden screams from Clara discovering the evidence of his crime. Next time, he decided, use tissues.

A few minutes later Jacob heard Clara's humming as it passed Katie's bedroom and faded down the stairs. Clara was oblivious to Jacob's presence, and even more oblivious to the show she just given him. Jacob's grin slowly faded into the silence that followed and he drifted to sleep. It didn't take long before he was snoring softly and dreaming once more of Clara.

Caught by Katie's Mom

Jacob opened his eyes and blinked away his sleep. He was staring at a pink ceiling so he knew he was in Katie's bed. Immediately his memories returned of watching Katie's mom, Clara, in the shower. He grinned thinking about Clara's naked body all glistening wet and covered in soap. Rolling over in bed he glanced at the alarm clock on Katie's nightstand. Was it nearly dinner time? *Dammit.* He hadn't meant to sleep that long, but after having the most intense orgasm of his life, he had to sleep.

Kicking his feet out of bed, Jacob sat up. He stretched and stifled a yawn. It was time to get ready for Katie's birthday party, he thought. She'll be home soon, and the least he could do was decorate. He found it difficult thinking about Katie when all his desires were for her mom. Yes, Clara was older, but thirty-four wasn't even approaching old in his books. He reasoned because Clara had kept in shape and ate healthy that she'd probably stay hot for years. His cock started getting hard as his mind replayed the images of watching Katie's mom in the shower. He felt a pang of remorse though. Not at what he'd done, but because he was probably never going to get another chance to spy on Clara like that again. Opportunities like that are once-in-a-lifetime.

Was it terrible to be fantasizing about Katie's mom? He wondered about it briefly. Clara seemed far sexier and more alluring than Katie ever did. Why was he was smitten with her? She was a fun outgoing woman, and for a mom, she was definitely a cool chick. He couldn't decide what exactly drove his sexual yearning for her though. All he knew was that he wanted more of her, but he had no idea how to make that happen. Spying on Clara naked in the shower was great fun, but he desperately wanted to feel those breasts in his hands, not just look at them.

Heading down to the kitchen, Jacob decided it was time to say hello. If Clara asked why he was there, he would be honest. Well, mostly honest. A little white lie never hurt anyone. There's no need to mention anything about spying on her in the shower. He'd say he had come over to decorate and must have fallen asleep. Then he'll apologize and fix her with his most charming smile. She'll probably smile and think it cute that her daughter's boyfriend was trying to be romantic, and with his busy work schedule, she'd understand how he could have fallen asleep. It sounded plausible enough. All will be forgiven and he could get on with decorating for Katie while secretly fantasizing about Clara. The reason he volunteered with the decorating in the first place was so he could be near Clara rather than to impress Katie. Sure it was a selfish ulterior motive, but it was true.

At the bottom of the staircase, Jacob paused and looked at himself in the mirror. His dark hair was a little unkempt and his shirt appeared a tad wrinkled. He quickly patted his hair and straightened his collar. No need to look like a bag of shit in front of Katie's mom, he thought. Satisfied with his appearance, Jacob turned and headed for the kitchen, putting on his best face.

"Hey, you're up!" Clara said as she looked up from her cutting. She had been chopping vegetables and storing them in little Tupperware containers for the party. She set the knife down on the cutting board, grabbed a hand towel and smiled at him. "Did you have a good snooze?"

"Oh, hey. Sorry yeah, I was tired. Hope you don't mind," Jacob said. He was caught off guard. How did she know he had been sleeping in Katie's bed? Did Clara also know he had spied on her while she showered? If so, she wasn't giving him any indication.

Clara nodded in understanding as she secured a clip on the bag of carrots and put them aside. He noticed she was wearing a pale blue summer dress that hung off her shoulders and flared at her hips. It looked good on her. Her long dark hair was pulled back in a scrunchy revealing her crisp jawline and delicate slender neck. Her skin was perfect, and her huge brown eyes sparkled when she smiled. She was so gorgeous, Jacob thought. Mentally he compared her body to Katie's as he watched her prepping for the party and decided he liked Clara's more. It wasn't even close.

Again he wondered if it was wrong to find an older woman attractive. She wasn't married, so it wasn't like he was moving in on her husband or threatening to break up the family. The story from Katie was that her mom accidentally got pregnant at fourteen and had Katie at fifteen. It was a bad break. The boy who knocked her up all those years ago was both long gone and long forgotten. Clara though persevered as a single mother and raised Katie on her own. An admirable thing for a teenager so young. Clara eventually got her high school diploma while changing diapers and then worked herself through college and earned her degree all the while making sure her daughter had everything a little girl needed. They were close, and Jacob knew he had to tread carefully.

So why the attraction to Katie's mom? Jacob had pondered this many times, and it didn't just come down to her great body. Lots of women had great bodies even younger women. Clara had a great personality he reasoned. She was fun and outgoing and seemed to have a natural aura of sexiness around her that wasn't manufactured or fake. Katie, on the other hand, was more reserved. She was still a great looking girl, but in Jacob's mind, nowhere near as sexy as her mom, nor fun to be around. Sexiness was the whole package, Jacob concluded. Not just good looks.

Clara poured a glass of orange juice and set it down. "Here, drink this. You look groggy and some juice is just the thing for you."

"Thank you, ma'am," Jacob said. He took a drink and smiled and then pulled out one of the kitchen bar stools and cautiously sat.

"And for the millionth time, just call me Clara. You make me feel old calling me ma'am this and ma'am that all the time." She handed him a coaster to put under his glass then went back to her cutting board.

Jacob wasn't suggesting she looked old, he was just being polite. *I just jerked off watching you in the shower. Trust me, you look great naked.* He felt nervous being this close to Clara. Her body was intoxicating to him, and her perfume only made it more so. He desperately needed to change the subject before he said something entirely stupid.

"So, when is Katie off work?"

Clara paused her cutting and looked at the wall clock. "She's done at eight, so if everything goes according to plan, she should be walking in that door about twenty after or so."

"Is there anything I can help you with?"

Clara puffed a strand of hair from her eyes as she looked around. She rubbed her nose with the back of her hand and continued slicing celery sticks. "Let's see, I need to hang the birthday banner after these are chopped. If you want, you can find me some tape in that drawer over there." She nodded towards the cupboards which released another strand of hair that fell across her face.

Jacob marvelled at how effortlessly gorgeous Clara was while he drank the last of his juice and set the cup down. When she cast a glance at the empty cup, he carefully picked it up and carried it to the sink. As he did so, he glanced at her backside, his mind flashing the image of her naked bottom through her dress like x-ray vision. He smiled. She had a great ass and too many times he'd imagined slapping it or sinking his cock into it. What would Clara think if she knew he had just spied on her in the shower?

He opened the drawer and picked up a roll of scotch tape.

"Great. Now grab the ladder in the garage. I'm almost done then we can do up some balloons too." She smiled and Jacob found himself wanting her. His mind kept flashing images of her naked body through her dress no matter how many times he tried not to.

"In the garage you said?"

"Yes, should be hanging up unless Katie forgot."

Jacob nodded and left the kitchen. When his back was turned, Clara looked up from her work and secretly admired his muscular body from behind. She particularly liked his shapely butt she thought with an appraising eye. Her mind warned her not to admire her daughter's boyfriend, but she couldn't help it. There was nothing wrong with an older woman admiring a finely bred younger man, was there?

When she had spotted him earlier sleeping in Katie's bed she was startled at first. She hadn't expected Jacob to be there. She guessed he was tired and must have fallen asleep waiting for Katie. How adorable. While gazing at Jacob sleeping, Clara wished briefly that there was a handsome man sleeping in her bed just waiting for her like that. She decided not to wake him, but she did steal a moment to admire his handsome face and strong body.

Too bad Katie was thinking of dumping the guy, Clara thought to herself as she resumed prepping for the party. Jacob, of course, didn't know. Katie had sworn Clara to secrecy when she first confessed her misgivings, and just wanted her mom's opinion on what she should do. When Clara expressed shock, Katie explained that she had met a new boy at college and was debating riding it out with Jacob until the end of summer or just break up now and pursue the other boy. Clara kept her thoughts to herself other than to suggest that Jacob was a handsome young man, and someday they might have good looking kids. This comment, of course, had sent Katie into apoplectic shock. She rolled her eyes at her mother and said that getting married and having kids was the last thing on her mind. Jacob was just a fling. Just a nice boy that she wasn't sure she wanted to commit her whole life to while she was young. Clara had smiled at that. She wouldn't mind a little fling with Jacob, but she knew her daughter would never forgive if she did. Still, there was no harm in admiring the boy.

Gathering the veggies, Clara stuffed them in the fridge. Despite Jacob's polite manners, she did get the impression that his eyes lingered on her a little too long from time to time. Most young men didn't stare at her like he often did. Sure there were the guys at the yoga studio (the man in the purple jumpsuit came to mind) or the odd dad in the supermarket that gave her an appraising glance or a lame one-liner in an effort to talk to her. But here in her own kitchen, she pondered whether Jacob had a crush on her. Call it female intuition.

Clara dried her hands and picked up the birthday banner before walking into the living room where she planned on having the surprise party. She wanted the birthday banner above the fireplace because the contrast would be perfect and you could see it right away when you walked in from the kitchen. The large coffee table and surrounding couches were already pushed back, leaving a large clear area in the middle of the room for everyone to gather and mingle.

Jacob returned carrying the ladder and asked where she wanted it set up. While admiring his muscles briefly, she pointed towards the fireplace. He was such a helpful young man, Clara thought, and that tight fitting shirt clung to his torso nicely. *If I was nineteen again, I would definitely date him.* Katie was young and lacked the appreciation Clara had in having such a helpful and well built young man around. Ah to be young again, Clara reminisced.

Holding the tape and banner in one hand, Clara directed Jacob's placement of the ladder. "A little to the left. That's it, perfect. Can I count on you to hold it steady for me? I don't want to fall."

Jacob smiled when he looked into her eyes. "I won't let you get hurt."

She liked his smile and didn't mind that his eyes briefly travelled down towards her cleavage. She didn't mind his admiration, but part of her wondered if he found her old and frumpy. Not that it mattered. Turning her attention to the ladder, Clara slowly climbed. At the second highest rung she glanced down at Jacob.

"Don't let me fall!" Clara said and then paused when she noticed him averting his eyes. *Was he peeking up my dress?* A thrill coursed through her at the sudden thought that Jacob might have been stealing a glance at her panties. Don't be silly Clara, she thought, it's just your imagination.

Clara liked her summer dress, but it suddenly became apparent that from where he was standing, Jacob had a clear view up her legs while she was on the ladder. She mentally tried to remember if she wore her sexy panties or her bloomers. *Oh please say he didn't see my giant bloomers.* Not bloomers, not bloomers she repeated in her mind. Her cheeks flushed. She turned her attention to hanging the birthday banner in an effort to hide her flushed face from him. The idea that he might be peeping up her skirt was thrilling in a way, but was it accidental or on purpose? Perhaps Jackie was right and I still have it.

When the edge of the banner was secured she quickly and purposely looked down. Her plan was to catch him staring but his head swivelled away expertly. It was confirmation enough, and Clara felt another thrill. *He was totally peeping!*

Pretending not to notice, she concealed her feelings and carefully climbed down the ladder with a poised face. Turning towards him, she smiled and said, "Thank you, now we need to move the ladder over... Are you okay?"

"What?"

"Jacob, your face is flushed. Are you feeling okay?"

Jacob cleared his throat his cheeks turning even more crimson. "No, I'm fine, thank you. It's the heat. I'm just allergic to the heat. It's a medical condition. Um, could I have a drink of water after we're done?"

She placed a hand on his muscular shoulder and nodded with concern. "Of course. I hope you aren't coming down with heat stroke or something in my very air conditioned house." Jacob failed to catch the sarcasm in her voice. "Katie is so looking forward to seeing you," she lied. Katie had no idea he was there. "You should lay down in my bed for a bit. I'll check on you later."

Jacob's flush travelled down his neck as he thought of being in Clara's bed.

"Did you know all of Katie's college friends are going to be here? I'd hate for you to miss the birthday party tonight. Maybe you should lie down."

"No thank you, just water," Jacob said. He moved the ladder to the new spot she indicated and held it firmly. Too firmly, she noticed with amusement.

When Clara climbed it a second time, she decided on impulse to lean forward and give him a show. The game was on, and she secretly enjoyed seeing the effect she had on him. She could feel his eyes on her and it thrilled her all over again. She didn't want to catch him—just tease him a little. It felt good to be desired by someone other than the creepy man in the purple tracksuit at yoga.

She purposely made a fuss adjusting the banner, making sure to turn this way and that so her dress swivelled. If he was going to peek up her dress, she might as well put on an innocent performance. Once satisfied, both with the banner and her impromptu show, she carefully stepped down and fixed Jacob with a sultry grin. His face was flushed. Perhaps even more flushed than before. She noticed a bulge in his pants, and it was her turn to blush. Young men can be so deliciously manipulated, she thought.

"I don't know what I'd do without such a strong man around," Clara said purposely placing a hand on his muscled chest and leaving it there. It was hard and unyielding. "Would you be so kind and put the ladder back in the garage?"

Jacob nodded dumbly but his eyes said it all. She could see his desire there. It was a harmless pleasure, giving him a little show. What man ever turned down peeping up a woman's skirt when given the opportunity? None.

Returning to the kitchen, Clara downed a glass of water. The house did feel warm she thought. Looking around she decided next to work on the final cake decorations. She glanced at the clock. She told Katie's college friends to arrive around seven. They would have to park all their cars at the neighbour's house or else Katie would know there was a surprise party before she even walked into the house. Clara had cleared it with her neighbour who thankfully had no problem converting their driveway into a temporary parking lot for the night.

When Jacob returned, his face had lost its flush. Clara glanced at him, looking for a hint of that lustful hunger she saw moments before. He looked somewhat frazzled, and when their eyes met, she could tell it was still there. For some reason, she felt relieved.

"I hung up the ladder. Is there anything else I can help you with?"

Clara regarded him a moment longer. "How about you run upstairs and take a shower? You look like you might be coming down with something. Are you sure you'll be okay for the party?"

"A shower?"

"Yes, you can use my shower," Clara said. "Do you know where it is?"

"I've... um... seen it before," Jacob said as his cheeks flushed and he abruptly turned away.

Clara frowned as Jacob retreated from the kitchen. What was that about? What an odd response. Why would he blush at the mention of using her shower? Did he think she was going to walk in on him? Who understood the mind of horny young men? Shrugging, she went back to preparing for the party.

* * *

Katie arrived home from work, feeling tired. She hadn't wanted to work on her birthday, but her boss insisted. Reluctantly she did her shift thinking her birthday was ruined. Now home, she walked in the door humming happy birthday to herself. She knew her mom would have bought some gifts, and maybe made a little cake, but what she really wanted was to see her friends. But the driveway was empty. No one came. Seeing the kitchen deserted made her heart sink even further. No one even remembered.

The happy birthday cries when she walked into the living room scared Katie so much that she nearly screamed. Caught completely off guard, she cried with happiness and clapped her hands. There were pink birthday cake plates and matching forks and even balloons. To her surprise, all her girlfriends did show up after all. Even Jacob was there smiling sheepishly in the corner next to her mom.

"You guys shouldn't have," Katie admonished them all with feigned severity, but in her heart, she was happy they hadn't forgotten her. It wasn't every day a girl turned nineteen.

* * *

Jacob didn't stay the night. He had hoped to, but it was clear from Katie's mannerisms and body language that he wasn't welcome. This was her night, and she wanted to spend it with her friends. He could respect that. So he had stayed for cake and presents and tried to chat up Katie's girlfriends but none of them gave him the time of day. He could tell when he wasn't welcome. Dejected, he decided to go home. Katie didn't even say goodnight. His only bright moment was when Clara intercepted him at the front door with a friendly thank you. She smelled good and looked even better. In that moment, Jacob regretted having to leave even more. Clara had no idea what he was feeling. She had no clue how badly he wanted just one night in bed with her. But that was just a fantasy. Who was he fooling?

When Clara leaned in for a thank-you hug, Jacob's heart quickened. He could feel her firm breasts press against his chest, and he sucked in his breath. It was a lingering hug and feeling her breasts pressed against him was the highlight of his night. Clara was probably not even aware that she had done it. To her boobs were boobs, probably. Clara was sexual without even being aware of it. She probably had no idea what her breasts did to him. He doubted sexual thoughts even crossed her mind. Not that he minded the feeling of her chest pressed against his own. With a heavy heart and the lingering smell of Clara's perfume in his mind, he wished Clara a good night, walked to his car and drove home.

* * *

The next morning was a new day. Refreshed and more determined than ever, Jacob, showered and shaved and eagerly drove over to Katie's house again. His plan was to spend quality alone time with Katie. He had been too caught up with this silly infatuation with Clara and it was time to put a stop to that. He needed a dose of reality. Clara wasn't at all interested in him, and never would. Women like Clara don't date their daughter's boyfriends. They have too much class.

Katie had seemed so distant lately and keeping his attention on Clara wasn't going to help. Today he would put all his focus on Katie, ignore Clara as best he could, and bridge that growing gap in their relationship.

For some reason he couldn't explain, Jacob pulled into the neighbour's driveway just as he had done the previous night. When he realised it he laughed. Well, I'm committed now, he thought and pulled up behind a collection of expensive sedans still there from the previous night. They were expensive cars he noticed, given to Katie's expensive friends by rich daddies who liked to spoil their daughters. No one ever bought him a car, but he wasn't bitter. Okay, just a little. He left enough room when he parked so the other cars could still get out. He doubted any of her friends would have had such thoughtful consideration for others.

Trudging over to Katie's house, Jacob felt his enthusiasm fade. He peered at the beautiful crystal blue ocean and wondered briefly that if things didn't work out with Katie, would it be considered bad taste to date her mother? Clara would never date a guy who was barely older than her own daughter. Would she? No, it was a stupid thought, and he rejected it at once, but his heart ached. A Thirty-four-year-old woman would have no interest in a twenty-year-old guy. He could never broach the topic, anyway. She would see his profession of love as an act of desperation. He felt trapped. At least it was a new day and he might get another smile from Clara. Better yet, another hug from her. He could briefly savour the pressure of her breasts pressed against him and savour her intoxicating perfume. It didn't hurt to dream, so long as he didn't put a voice to thought.

The front door was locked. He laughed. Of course, it was locked. Jacob fished for his key and unlocked the door. Stepping inside he turned and locked the deadbolt and then glanced towards the kitchen. No one was there. He could see evidence of breakfast dishes and detect the smell of cooking in the air. By the look of things, it seemed everyone was up at least. But where were they?

Walking into the living room he glanced at the remnants of the party feeling a pang of disappointed. He hadn't felt very welcome the night before, but did that really matter? Did he want the approval of spoiled girls? It would have been nice to stay longer at least, but Katie wanted to be with her girlfriends.

Glancing at the table he noticed a lot of left-over cake. He knew rich girls seldom ate birthday cake, at least not when others could see and judge them. It would ruin their perfectly crafted bodies and destroy their carefully crafted images. Katie's friends were all obsessed with proper diets and eating cake was just not done. He could have told Clara that. Frowning, he thought he probably should have mentioned it and saved her time. No one eats birthday cake, at least not rich girls.

"Where the hell is everyone?" Jacob said while looking around the empty living room. He then heard splashing and laughter. The pool? Are they in the pool?

Heading towards the back of the house Jacob peered through the blinds. He could see five of Katie's girlfriends who stayed the night. They were lounging in the sun and splashing around in the pool. He spotted Katie in a skimpy pink bikini talking to her mom. He couldn't help but enjoy the arousing quality of so many girls revealing so much tanned skin. Rich girls or not, he had to admit they did have hot bodies. Probably from not eating cake, he thought with a grin.

They didn't know he was in the house peering at them through the blinds. The girls and Clara thought they were alone. He should probably just go outside and say hello... but then again.

A thrill ran up his spine. It was the same thrill he felt watching Clara in the shower only a day ago. Why did spying on beautiful women unawares thrill him like this? He attributed it to voyeuristic excitement. Observing a woman with her guard down revealed a lot about her. They don't know they're being observed, so they act differently, more naturally he guessed. They also can't glare or slap your face if your gaze lingers too long over a shapely breast or on the curve of a firm ass. You can examine any part of a girl for as long as you want without the social awkwardness of explaining yourself. The girl being spied on doesn't try to hide her imperfections or cover her body in private. From a secret place, you can see anything and everything on display without the slightest hindrance. Whatever it was, the power was sexually intoxicating. He felt a stir in his pants as his cock grew hard.

Jacob considered opening the sliding door and greeting everyone. That would be the sensible thing to do—the right thing to do. But then the girls might cover themselves, or act more reserved and he would lose the chance to enjoy the view in more detail. He could always take care of business first and then show himself. He liked that choice better. None of the girls would be any the wiser, and besides, he reasoned, no one would be harmed. It's not like he was being a pervert or anything. He just wanted to use them as visual stimulation.

Clara had rooms upstairs that overlooked the pool, didn't she? The more he thought, the more the idea of taking care of business intrigued him. From the privacy of an upstairs room, he could freely jerk off, enjoying all bikini-clad girls frolicking in the sun. It would be a visual feast. It would be exhilarating for sure, and with a grin, Jacob decided to find out. An opportunity like this was rare. He pulled back from the window, careful not to disturb the blinds and quickly darted through the kitchen and climbed the marble staircase.

What room would be best? Jacob hurried into Clara's bedroom and peered carefully from her balcony. The view of the pool was obscured by tall hedges. That was no good. The entire pool area was enclosed with privacy bushes, preventing anyone except those from the upper floors of the house to see any of it. He needed another room.

Backtracking, Jacob walked past Katie's bedroom. He had to find something facing the back of the house, and Katie's room faced the front. The first door he opened revealed a sewing room. *Clara had a sewing room?* Interesting, he thought. Ah right, her interior decorating business. A table and piles of fabrics stacked against the window blocked most of the view. He decided to check the other rooms. There had to be something better.

Picking the second master bedroom next, he opened the door. He had never been in this part of the house before. It appeared that Clara had converted the spacious room into an office for her business. Papers, drawings, and rolls of fabric covered her desk. This was a much better choice, and besides it was Clara's space, so it added to his excitement of jerking off in a place where she spent so much of her time. He approached the window and parted the Venetian blinds. There was a perfect view of the entire pool area. He grinned. Everyone was still frolicking around the pool with no one the wiser that his hungry eyes watched them. Now all he needed was a handful of tissues and some lotion...

* * *

"Hey mom, we're going topless," Katie said, enjoying her mom's startled reaction. "Want to join us?"

"Are you now? Aren't you afraid the neighbours will see?"

Katie gestured at the impenetrable hedges to show what she thought of that possibility. "We're working on our tans. Come on, it'll be fun!"

Clara felt foolish. She looked at Katie's friends who were already peeling off their bikini tops and she smiled. She missed feeling young again. As tempting as it was to relax in the sun topless, she really had to get the house tidied up from the party.

"I'll pass," Clara said, fixing her daughter with an amused grin. "You and your friends enjoy yourselves. I'm going in to tidy up, but I'll play lookout. If any dastardly men arrive, I promise to sound the alarm and protect your virtue."

Katie laughed and then stepped closer and hugged her. "Thanks, mom, you're the coolest."

"Have fun girls!" Clara shouted. At least I'm cool, she thought to herself. She collected empty glasses and walked towards the sliding door. "Katie, could you get that for me, honey?"

Katie darted ahead and grabbed the door. "No problem, mom, and thanks." Once she closed the door, Katie turned towards her friends. They were all watching her expectantly. Fixing a mischievous grin on her face, she pulled the drawstring on her bikini top and yanked. It felt good to expose her bare breasts. Liberating.

Her friends laughed as the usually reserved Katie ran towards the pool, flung her bikini top and launched herself high into the air. Her friends shrieked and applauded when Katie performed a thunderous cannonball in the middle of the pool. With shrieks of liberation, her friends got up and joined her, diving or jumping or making cannonballs of their own. Soon everyone was laughing and splashing with carefree abandon, bikini tops strewed about.

Clara set the empty glasses on the kitchen counter and briefly surveyed the collection of dirty breakfast dishes. She then walked into the living room and retrieved the cake and frowned because it was mostly uneaten. Setting it on the counter she scooped an edge of frosting and plopped it in her mouth. She stared at the cake perplexed. So much time was wasted decorating it and hardly anyone ate any. Next year, she decided, if she threw another birthday party for Katie, she'd make a healthy alternative instead.

Rinsing her hands under the tap, Clara glanced through the kitchen window out towards the driveway. Jacob's car wasn't there. Part of her hoped he would drop by for a visit. She grabbed a tea towel and dried her hands. Walking to the front door she double checked the lock.

Part of her doubted Jacob would show. He seemed pretty dejected last night, she thought. Katie wasn't brushing him off or anything, but Clara could definitely read her daughter's body language. She was at the undecided stage of her relationship with Jacob, so naturally kept her distance from him. The poor fellow looked like a lost puppy most of the night. It was nice giving him a hug, though, Clara mused. She wasn't used to touching something so hard and chiselled as Jacob's body. She sighed. In thirty years will Katie look back with regret? Will Katie wonder what her life would have been like with a boy like Jacob? Clara hated to see such a fine young man thrown to the curb. Her daughter seemed determined to chase a phantom mystery boy from college instead of being thankful for the young man she had now. Katie did seem fickle, Clara thought. She was always chasing the next shiny thing. It didn't surprise Clara to see that her daughter had commitment issues with boys. She grew up knowing her own mother was abandoned by a guy who had professed his love and commitment once Clara was pregnant but then ran away. Katie grew up without a father, and Clara could see how it colored her relationships now. Maybe subconsciously, Katie was afraid that Jacob would leave her, so to protect herself, she leaves him first and chases the next one. It could develop into a vicious cycle, but she had to let her daughter work things out on her own.

A sound from upstairs caught her attention. Standing still, Clara tilted her head and perked her ears. There it was again. It sounded like a drawer being opened and then closed. Was there a burglar in the house? Was that one of Katie's friends? Carefully moving through the kitchen, she peered out back and did a quick head count. All of Katie's friends were accounted for–and topless. There shouldn't be anyone upstairs. Alarm filled her. Should she call the police? Should she warn the girls to cover themselves? What if it was nothing?

On impulse, she headed towards the marble staircase and stopped at the bottom. With a hand on the railing, she craned her neck and listened. Nothing. Maybe it was the wind? The Wind doesn't open and close drawers she reminded herself. After a few minutes of silence, Clara tentatively climbed the marble staircase. At the top, she paused and cocked her head. There was nothing. Not a sound. The bathroom light was on. Was that light on before? She couldn't recall. Stopping in the hallway, she peered in. Nothing seemed out of place and all the drawers were closed. Next, she checked Katie's room. It was empty too. Had it just been her imagination? She checked her own room just for peace of mind and found no intruders. She let out a breath she hadn't realised she was holding.

Feeling relieved, Clara turned towards the stairs. The sound must have been her imagination playing tricks.

Glancing down the hallway, she noticed that the door to her office was open. Stopping in her tracks, she did a double-take. She never left her office door open. She blinked and stared, feeling her heart begin to thump against her chest. Controlling her breathing, Clara tried to calm her nerves. What were the telltale signs of a burglar? Perhaps someone rummaging through her desk might make a noise, perhaps knock something over in their haste to find valuables. She held very still and listened. One minute passed. Then two. Had one of Katie's friends accidentally wandered in there earlier and just forgotten to close the door? Possibly, but she had done a head count, she reminded herself, and everyone was accounted for. I really ought to take a self-defense course. Why did I waste time doing yoga when I need to learn karate?

No one was in her office it seemed. Maybe she had just left the door open and was getting worked up over nothing. Obviously, the only way to find out was to check. But in her heart, she didn't want to check. Clara thought of her daughter's safety. Determined, she started slinking towards the open door, ready at the first sign of trouble to turn and make a run for the stairs. At the threshold to her office, she stopped, held her breath, and listened.

There was a sound!

Her heart raced, and she listened closer. There it was again. Yes, there was definitely a sound, but not a sound she recognised. It was a steady sound, almost rhythmic. That was puzzling. To Clara, it sounded like someone rubbing their hands together with sanitizer foam. Confused, Clara peered ever so slowly into the room. What she saw not only startled her but nearly made her cry in astonishment.

Jacob, naked from the waist down, was standing with his back to her, furiously jerking off while peering through the window blinds. The rhythmic sound was from him stroking his cock. Clasping a hand over her mouth, Clara took a moment to suppress her shock. In the meantime she stared as Jacob continued to jerk off, clenching his butt cheeks and thrusting his hips as if imagining sex with one of the girls below. Her mind tried to process what her eyes were seeing. He hadn't noticed her, so she had a moment to think. Do all men talking dirty while masturbating? Curious now, she listened and had to stop herself from laughing. He was coaching the girls around the pool with words like, 'Oh baby' and 'Just like that'. The little sneaky devil.

She had to admit this was the first time she ever saw such a thing, other than when Steve had done it at the yoga studio. But Steve was more gentle with himself. Jacob appeared more animalistic, accompanying his jerking motions with grunts and odd sounds. It looked harsh and painful and not at all pleasant. She noticed on the corner of the desk beside him, a wad of toilet paper and a bottle of hand lotion. *Hey, that's my hand cream! Gross!*

Clara tore her eyes from what she was seeing and retreated into the hallway to collect her thoughts. He wasn't aware that she had caught him in the act. Should she confront him? Maybe yell something from the bottom of the stairs and scare him? She could retreat to the bathroom and make a lot of noise; maybe pretend to shout something downstairs or flush the toilet. He would hear that and stop. On the other hand if she just went back to the kitchen she could pretend she never saw anything. Unfortunately certain things in life, once seen, cannot be unseen. This was one of those moments.

What to do, what to do? Should I act like it never happened? What would Katie think? No, she couldn't let him use the girls as a visual aid to masturbation. There had to be something she could do. There was no way he was going to get away with this, Clara decided firmly. You don't play peeping Tom in my house and get away with it!

She needed advice. Clara wondered briefly what Jackie would do in a situation like this. She knew right away what her friend would do. Join him probably. That idea did have some appeal. Clara smiled as a naughty thought crossed her mind. Perhaps she could teach Jacob a lesson and also enjoy herself in the process? That choice sounded much more appealing. If she confronted him, then there would be leverage. Blackmailing leverage. He would be mortified would he not? Terrified that she might call the police, or worse, reveal his dirty masturbating secret to Katie and her friends. The girls would ridicule him before tearing him apart. He would be humiliated and probably end up in the hospital too. Katie would be disgusted and break up with him on the spot. He wouldn't want that. Clara realised she didn't want that either. If they broke up, then she couldn't enjoy Jacob around the house. She couldn't admire his body or flirt with him.

Clara knew that if she simply warns him of her presence, then any leverage would be lost. He would stop, clean up quickly and deny everything. She had to catch him in the act so there was no misunderstanding of their new power dynamic. But how do you confront a man who is jerking off like a deranged monkey?

An idea popped into her mind and Clara grinned. She quietly walked back into the room and crept up behind Jacob. He was staring so intently through the blinds that he still hadn't noticed her. She observed him for a moment, finding the sight both fascinating and disturbing at the same time. She was mere feet away from a handsome young man masturbating and felt a little aroused.

As curious as she was watching him, it was time to put an end to this. Clara folded her arms, assumed a stern expression and cleared her throat with purpose.

Jacob's head whirled at the sound and his eyes bulged in terror. He doubled over in a panic and covered his cock with both hands, and then desperately started looking for his shorts and boxers. They were draped over the back of the office chair, and out of reach.

Clara looked him up and down, made a clearly disgusted sound, and started tapping her foot. "What in the hell do you think you're doing in here?"

"Shit! Oh, my god, I'm so sorry!" Jacob tried to shrink from her like she was sunlight piercing the clouds and he was a vampire caught outside. His face turned bright red, and he averted his eyes as the full shock of being discovered began to sink in. This was the most embarrassing moment of his life. Being caught jerking off was bad enough, but being caught by the one woman in the world he wanted to impress was a disaster. Any chance he might have had with Clara just turned to dust. He made a desperate arm swing to grab his shorts, but they remained out of reach.

"Don't you dare move," Clara said sternly. She fixed him with a strict dominating glare that said she wasn't kidding. Jacob shirked from her gaze and froze.

"I'm sorry, oh my god I'm so sorry," Jacob sobbed. "Please, it's not what you think!"

Tilting her head, Clara's eyes bore into him. "I think this is exactly what I think it is. You were staring outside at my daughter and her friends and you were masturbating, in my office, in my house, and with my hand lotion."

"Please, I'm sorry. Don't... Oh God, please don't... just don't tell Katie. I'm so sorry. I'll go now. Let me go home, please."

Clara made another disgusted sound and walked around Jacob to the window. She parted the blinds and peered out, her brown eyes sharp and angry. All the girls were topless. From her office window, Jacob had had a perfect view, and the privacy to masturbate all he wanted. In her office. Looking at her daughter. She fumed as the disrespect of it all began to sink in. Oh, he was going to be punished. It was something he would never forget, Clara promised herself. Out of the corner of her eye, she noticed his arm discretely reaching for his shorts.

Clara whirled on him. "I said don't move. Do you think this is some sort of game young man? This is my house, and my office and that is my daughter outside. Is this a regular habit of yours, this jerking off while watching my daughter?"

"What? No! Never. I never... no. This is my first time. I'm so sorry."

She looked down at his hands covering his cock. So he likes to look at topless girls? Let's see how he likes being looked at, she thought in anger.

"Remove your hands," Clara ordered.

"Pardon?"

"I said, move your hands. I'm sure Katie's seen it a hundred times, but I want to see what you were doing. Stop slouching and stand up straight for god sakes. Good boy," Clara said as he slowly straightened. "Now do as I say and move your hands."

Jacob froze like a deer in the headlights. He was too terrified to move his hands and too ashamed to show his erect cock. He stared at Clara with a face full of incomprehension. His mind tried desperately to process the situation. Why did she want to see it? Wasn't catching him in the act bad enough, now she had to humiliate him? When she raised an eyebrow he relented, the fear of her anger overpowering his fear of revealing himself. Looking away, he reluctantly moved his hands and waited for her laughter.

But Clara didn't laugh. To her, his cock looked impressive. He missed the momentary surprise on her face when she saw its length and girth. Clara felt her cheeks flush and her body respond. Was this arousal from the sight of his cock or the power she held over him? Did it matter? She couldn't remember how long it was since she last saw a young man's cock, so strong and so hard. Too long, she realised.

"Have you had sex with my daughter?"

"What? No never ma'am. Honest truth."

"Show me what you were doing. I want to see," Clara ordered. She felt a tingle of arousal at the expression that crossed his hapless face.

"Pardon me ma'am? You want me to do what? I... don't understand."

Placing hands on her hips, Clara nodded towards the window. "Show me what you were doing. You know, continue. I want to watch."

"You mean keep going?" Jacob's mind raced. "You want me to do what I was doing again? I'm confused, aren't you mad or something?"

"I haven't decided if I'm angry or not. Besides, you are not in a position to be asking questions here. Now I'm not going to ask again. Now get back to that window and finish. I want to see you doing it. We'll talk about proper punishments later. Understand?"

Wearily Jacob returned to the window. She watched as he self-consciously gripped his cock and started fiddling with it. Casting a last confused glance at Clara, he turned his head and peered through the blinds at the topless girls around the pool. He focused on Katie as she sat on the side of the pool with her legs in the water. She was kicking and splashing and from the window, Jacob could see her firm breasts shake and jiggle. His cock began to respond and grow harder in his hand.

He tried to ignore the fact that he was in a world of trouble as Clara stepped closer and looked down at what he was doing to himself. He felt embarrassed and his cheeks burned with humiliation but for some reason having Clara watching him, spurred his cock to new life. It didn't take him long to realize it wasn't the topless girls that were exciting him, as he stroked, it was Clara. He was turned on by her presence.

"Interesting," Clara said, then bit her lip softly. She was getting wet.

"Please ma'am this is humiliating. Don't make me—"

"Hush!" Clara snapped. "Don't talk and ruin this. You didn't have any problem jerking off before I busted you, so continue doing it."

Jacob took a determined breath and peered back through the window. Two of Katie's friends drew his attention. They had climbed out of the pool and turned to face the house, unaware he was watching them. It looked like they were wringing out their hair. He watched their slender tanned bodies bend over as they collected their hair then flung it back. While the girls fussed his eyes devoured their bare breasts. He felt his cock tingle. He varied his stroke, not sure if he was supposed to finish or not, or just demonstrate. The whole experience was surreal and if he wasn't careful, he was going to cum soon.

Jacob, face flushed, turned and looked at Clara. "I'm close... what should I do?"

Tilting her head, Clara thought for a moment. She scooped the wad of toilet paper and handed it to him. "I'm guessing this is what you planned to use originally?"

Jacob felt stupid thanking her as he took the tissues from her hand. She pointedly indicated that he was to continue, her brown eyes focused and her face marked with interest. He could see her cheeks were flushed a little. Was she enjoying this? He continued to stroke his cock. Normally jerking off in front of Clara would be a huge fantasy for him, but not now. Without knowing if he was in serious trouble or not, it just felt strange. His dream had finally come true, and he was terrified of displeasing her.

"I want to see you finish. Do you like to masturbate while watching my daughter and her friends? Don't stop. Eyes out the window, Jacob. Now finish and make it good. Impress me."

Swallowing hard, Jacob held the tissue ready and stroked harder. He doubted what he was about to do would impress anyone. He felt his balls twitch. A tingle ran up his shaft. She was standing so close he could smell her perfume. He shut his eyes and imagined that Clara was kneeling on the floor with an upturned face desperately wanting him to cum all over it. Who wouldn't want to cum on that gorgeous face and cover it with thick gobs of cream? He was almost there. Jacobs mind flashed to Clara in the shower. It was much more stimulating, the memory still fresh. She was on her knees in this fantasy, her mouth open desperately begging him to cum. Jacob opened his eyes. Clara was standing right beside him watching, her eyes staring at his hard cock. Just knowing she would see him orgasm pushed him over the edge.

With a grunt, Jake buried the head of his cock in the wad of toilet paper and turned to stare at Clara while jerking himself furiously. She seemed surprised when he looked at her and her eyes went wide. She wasn't expecting such intensity. He groaned in pleasure as his cock erupted. It was a violent and powerful orgasm fueled by her closeness. His muscular body twitched and convulsed as his cock emptied but he never took his eyes off her beautiful face.

"Do you do this often? Stare at girls and masturbate?" Clara asked feeling overly aroused and flushed herself now. Her mind was filling with possibilities and desire. She had to have that cock in her. She wanted him to stare at her with that hungry intensity again. She wanted to wrap her legs around him and feel his cock explode inside of her while she climaxed. Clara almost gasped when it suddenly became clear in her mind; she wanted to fuck Jacob.

"No ma'am. I'm sorry. I should have known better. Please don't tell Katie about this. Please," Jacob said. He felt spent.

"That all depends on you now doesn't it?" Clara said, regaining her composure. "How long until you can do that again?"

"Pardon ma'am?"

"Never mind," Clara said with a shake of her hand. "Clean up and get dressed, you look pathetic standing there with your dick in your hand. Be downstairs in five minutes." She turned to go but paused and looked over her shoulder. "And stop calling me ma'am. I thought we went over that already."

Jacob watched in bewilderment as she cast an appraising look at his spent cock and then spun on her heel and walked out of the room. He stood alone and looked around. "What the hell just happened?" he said.

* * *

Once Jacob had cleaned up and composed himself he paused at the top of the stairs. Getting caught was definitely not his plan. He needed to be careful now. Clara held all the cards. Would she reveal what she just found him doing to Katie and her friends? He really didn't know. One thing was certain; Clara wasn't about to let this crime go unpunished. He could see it in her eyes. Why did she insist he finish? Wasn't it a little strange that she wanted to watch him jerk off? Was that meant to be a punishment for him or was it a curiosity for her? Perhaps Clara was a bit of a freak herself. Instead of being outraged and offended when she caught him, she seemed to enjoy it. What was her plan? Jacob had no idea how he was going to get out of this mess.

Whatever happened, he would just have to face it. There was no choice really but take it like a man. He already fucked up any hope he ever had of hooking up with Clara, so there was no point pretending anymore. He would take his lumps. Worrying now won't change his fate. Grabbing his courage, Jacob descended the stairs. He could hear a few of the girls in from the pool and felt a pit of dread forming in his stomach. He felt like a man walking to his own execution.

He spotted Clara in the kitchen. She was casually pouring orange juice for the girls. She glanced at him as he cautiously lowered himself on the kitchen stool. What she was thinking? He had no idea, but she did hand him a glass of juice. He couldn't read her expression when he took the glass from her hand. He was caught, and they both knew it. Like a criminal awaiting trial, he tried to look as harmless as possible for the judge and jury. Perhaps if he looked repentant, the sentence might be lenient. He doubted Clara was going to be lenient with him, but he had to try.

"Jacob!" Katie exclaimed walking into the kitchen. Jacob jumped and nearly dropped his glass. She rushed over and threw her arms around him. "When did you get here? You missed our morning swim."

No, I didn't. He glanced at Clara with guilt on his face. She was watching him now; reading him. Perhaps waiting to pass divine judgement if he misspoke?

Jacob cleared his throat. "I just got here," he said. "How's the birthday girl?"

"Tired, but happy," Katie said with a laugh and gave him another hug.

A gaggle of Katie's friends strolled into the kitchen. They had their tops back on Jacob noticed. He buried his face in his drink and could see Clara out of the corner of his eye. She seemed to be smirking now but thankfully remained silent. If she was going to announce his crime to everyone, it didn't appear it would be right away. There was some breathing room. How long was she going to delay judgement though? If her plan was to make him squirm and suffer, it was working.

"There is nothing more liberating than a morning dip in the pool. Wouldn't you agree with me, girls?" Katie said with a wink to her friends. There were grins and tinkles of laughter.

"We're all heading into town," Katie said, turning to Jacob.

"Oh?"

"Doing girl shopping. Do you want to come?"

Jacob caught the warning on Clara's face. It was barely perceptible, but he saw it. He smiled at Katie and shook his head. "No, I think I'll just stay here and help your mom clean up. Besides, I have to work later. You go and have a good time."

Katie's face turned thoughtful. "I thought you had the day off?"

"Oh, yeah someone called in sick. You know how these things are," Jacob lied. He glanced again at Clara and received the barest of nods.

"Well, suit yourself," Katie said. She downed her orange juice and tossed her mom a smile before bounding out of the room, her friends in tow.

Jacob noticed not one of her rich snobby friends even said hello to him. He hated spoiled brats and fought the urge to admire their bikini-clad bottoms as they walked away. They might have great bodies, but he was aware of his recent crime and Clara's gaze on him. Best not be ogling girls right now, he thought. Instead, he focused on the countertop as Katie and her friends went upstairs. When they were gone, he looked up. Clara was regarding him silently, but she had a particularly strange expression.

Jacob tried to look meek and casual but felt guilt all over his face. Part of him wished she would just chew him out and banish him forever. She was making him nervous.

Unable to take her gaze or his guilt, Jacob tried defiance. "What?"

"Don't think I've forgotten," Clara said quietly.

Jacob blinked, acutely aware of his shame. "I don't think I ever will."

Tapping a finger on her chin, Clara thought for a moment. "You can start with the cleaning the living room, and then the pool area. I want these dishes cleaned and put away. This is only the start of your punishment, Jacob. Trust me, there will be more. A lot more."

Punishments? He peered at the mess of plates, forks, and cups in the sink. So her plan for punishment was chores? He thought about her request. He could do chores if that was what she wanted. She held all the cards, anyway. He nodded and decided to take his lumps like a man.

"Okay, I think I get it," Jacob said while slowly getting to his feet.

She was licking her lips suggestively. He had never seen her act overtly sexual to him and he gulped. He suddenly felt like he was in the presence of a hunting cat. Not a house cat, though, but one of those big cats like a leopard. Jacob had the distinct feeling he had gone from hunter to prey. Her face suddenly brightened, though, and she gave him a coy smile.

"Oh, you have no idea," Clara said in a husky tone that caught his eye.

"About what?" Jacob asked wearily. He didn't know if he should be afraid or excited. He wanted to see her licking her lips again.

"Your punishments have just begun young man. When my daughter and her friends leave," Clara said, pushing her breasts together with her arms as she leaned closer, "I'm going to take a shower. You better have things tidied up if you want to join me."

"Join you?" Jacob gasped unable to look away from her revealing cleavage.

"You heard me," Clara said and suppressed a laugh. It only took a moment for comprehension to show on his face. His eyes grew wide, and he stared at her questioning. Clara nodded and once again licked her lips as she slowly peeled a dress strap off her shoulder and let it hang on her arm.

Jacob quickly grabbed a broom and bolted from the room. He had never wanted to clean so fast in his life. The sound of Clara's laughter followed him.

Punished by Katie's Mom

"Oh look, your manservant is cleaning," one of Katie's friends snorted.

Jacob looked up from his work stuffing used paper plates and plastic forks from Katie's birthday party into a garbage bag. Katie and her five college friends had walked into the kitchen from the backyard pool and stood looking at him.

"Hey there," Jacob said dryly, noticing the girls had changed out of their skimpy bikinis and now wore designer shorts and t-shirts. Jacob thought the snorters name might be Tiffany, but he wasn't sure. Katie had never introduced *that* friend to him. It didn't matter, though, he disliked Snorter anyway.

Tiffany the Snorter smacked her chewing gum while twirling a finger around her hair. She looked at him with disdain, much the same way medieval royalty might look down at a peasant in the mud.

"Katie?" Snorter continued, "When the manservant is done cleaning the kitchen please have him wash my clothes."

Katie slapped her arm in jest. "Don't be such a meanie. I think it's sweet he's helping. Thank you, Jacob."

Scooping up the last plastic fork and dropping it into the bag, Jacob shot Snorter a taunting; she thinks I'm adorable so nyah nyah look, and thought *I've seen your tits Tiffany, and I know they're fake. I enjoyed them while I jerked off.*

"Honey, please come shopping? I feel like we never get to spend time together," Katie said. Her tone seemed patronizing. She had no wish for Jacob to tag along, and he knew that. She just wanted to put on a good show for her friends.

Jacob waved his hand dismissively. "Nah, I'm good. Just bought me a brand-new wardrobe a few weeks ago." He hadn't, but it sounded good. "I just stopped by to kill time before I gotta get to work later. I'll catch ya tonight, maybe."

Tiffany, unable to resist one last dig, looked at his clothes before turning towards her friends. "New wardrobe? I didn't know we had a Salvation Army in San Altra."

Jacob said nothing as he smirked, which annoyed Tiffany even more.

"Stop that," Katie said and rolled her eyes. She uttered an exasperated sigh and turned towards Jacob. "Okay, have fun, I'll miss you!"

Jacob leaned in for a goodbye kiss, but Katie sidestepped, grabbing her purse and keys off the counter and heading for the door before he could plant one.

Tiffany turned and flicked her hair. "You missed a spot."

"Bitch," Jacob said under his breath. Hearing Katie's friends laugh and enjoy themselves made him jealous, and he didn't know why. They were annoying, plastic girls, at best, and he was growing tired of them. When the last lemming shut the door, Jacob shook his head and rinsed the dishcloth under the tap.

Returning to more pleasant thoughts, Jacob wondered about Clara once more. Why had Katie's mom asked him to join her in the shower? Were they going to have sex? He hoped so, and now that his girlfriend was gone, the opportunity was there. He wanted it badly, but he doubted that would ever happen with Clara.

Never in the history of time has any mom who caught a man masturbating to her daughter, ever turned around and rewarded that man with sex. It just didn't happen–ever. He knew any chance of scoring with Clara (before she caught him masturbating) was gone now. On the other hand, if there was no chance for sex, then why tell him to join her in the shower?

He gave the countertop one last wipe and scanned for anything he missed. Satisfied, he rinsed the dishcloth once more and wrung it out. Clara would be impressed, he thought. So why did he feel so nervous?

A few minutes later Clara did appear. She stood in the kitchen and looked around. Jacob smiled expectantly, but she ignored him. Instead, she examined the spotless counter with barely a nod. Next, she inspected the living room next. All the furniture from the party was returned to their rightful places.

"I know it might not be up to your standards," Jacob said surveying his work, "but did I do a good job?"

"Only speak when spoken to," Clara said in a curt tone, turning to look at him for the first time. She stuck a finger in his chest. "All men should learn that rule. Has Katie, and the girls left? I thought I heard the front door close."

"You just missed them," Jacob said helpfully. "Like by five minutes or so."

"Have you finished cleaning or do I need to inspect the pool area?"

"No, I got all that too," Jacob said proudly.

"Good. It took you long enough," Clara said without a smile. "I'm going upstairs to take a shower. You may follow."

"Can I ask a question first?"

Clara felt annoyed; he was talking again. She nodded with reluctance.

"What happened earlier... upstairs, I mean. I know you're pretty upset and all, but I'm confused. You asked me to clean up after the party, and I guess that's part of my punishment and all. But does an invitation to shower with you mean my punishment is over?"

"Young man," Clara said, running a finger down the side of his cheek. "What you did upstairs was reprehensible. Don't think, even for a moment, that your punishment is over. Consider this as a small reward for being obedient. You see, I like to reward obedient slaves sometimes. But, my dear pet, your lessons are only just beginning."

Slaves? Lessons? Jacob was still confused, and it showed on his face. Clara ignored it. Turning on a heel, she walked towards the marble staircase only pausing briefly to see that Jacob was following. He was. She disguised a small smile as she mounted the steps.

Once in her bedroom, she turned and glanced at Jacob. He had stopped in her doorway and was standing nervously, his eyes wide with apprehension. Clara tried to ignore how handsome he was.

"Take off your clothes." She pointed to her bed. "Put them there, folded."

Jacob hesitated for a moment and then shrugged with a grin. He peeled off his top and slipped his shorts and boxers down. Clara watched as he scooped his clothes and dumped them on her bed.

"Folded, I said. Were you born in a barn?"

"Sorry," Jacob blurted. He carefully folded his clothes and arranged them in a neat pile. "How's that?"

"How's that, *who*?" Clara asked with a raised eyebrow.

"How's that, ma'am?"

"Mistress," Clara stated.

"Mistress." Jacob corrected himself.

"In private, you will address me as Mistress. But you will *not* speak unless asked a specific question. I have no interest in your juvenile thoughts. Is that understood?"

Jacob scratched his head. He could learn to enjoy a little role playing, he thought. Deciding he liked where this was going, he nodded.

"Yes, Mistress."

"I'm glad we cleared that up. Now, there will be a few rules. I assume even a dimwit like you will you be able to follow them? I need to know if you can follow my rules, or else you may leave, and I will shower alone."

Jacob wondered what sort of rules she wanted. Was she referring to calling her Mistress and not talking? He guessed there were new rules. "Can I hear these rules before I agree to them?"

"No, you may not."

Okay, he thought, there were new rules. But she wasn't going to tell him unless he agreed with a blank cheque? He decided that all games had rules. He'd just pick them up as he went along. Clara could make whatever silly rules she wanted, so long as he got to see her naked again. If this was Clara's idea of foreplay before sex, then he would give her a blank cheque.

"I promise, Mistress."

"While in the shower, you will stand obediently. You will not talk. You will not ask questions. You will not touch yourself. And most importantly, you will not touch me unless instructed. Is that understood?"

Jacob's cock was starting to rise. Clara fought her urge to stare at it. Ogling his cock would ruin the authority she was trying to establish over the naked hot-blooded young male standing before her.

"I think I can do all that."

"You think?" Clara raised an eyebrow. "Perhaps I've made a mistake." She turned to leave, making it clear what she thought of his indecision.

"No! No mistake, Clara! I mean, Mistress. I can follow rules," Jacob said in a rush, interrupting her.

Clara regarded him for a moment and then nodded. She turned around and lifted her hair. "You may undo my dress. No touching."

Whatever the game, Jacob was willing to play along. He obediently worked the zipper down, revealing her smooth, flawless skin. She hadn't commanded him to do anything else, so he stopped, and then remembering her rule, remained silent as well. This foreplay felt very sensual, Jacob thought. He couldn't wait to fuck her.

Turning, Clara faced him. "Keep your eyes on my face only." She made sure he obeyed her instructions. Satisfied, she slipped her dress off her shoulders letting it fall to her ankles.

Jacob couldn't help but smirk slightly. He liked her form of foreplay. He was willing to do whatever it took to get her in the mood, but he had to be patient. This game seemed to have a lot of rules. But the prize was worth it. Once his cock was inside her, he would be victorious, win the game, and then fuck her brains out. That's all that mattered.

"Keep your eyes on my face," Clara said once again, making sure he clearly understood her wishes. He appeared to, so she reached behind her back and unhooked her bra. Bringing the straps down her arms, Clara peeled it away leaving her crossed arms covering her bare breasts.

Jacob's cock twitched. He wanted to look, but he forced himself not to. Instead, he kept his eyes locked on her smoldering brown eyes. He wanted to show her that he could play her game. Besides, he had seen her breasts already, so he could resist his urges for a few more minutes if it made her happy enough to fuck him.

Satisfied that Jacob was controlled and obeying, Clara tucked her thumbs into her panties and wiggled them over her hips. They pooled around her ankles before she kicked them away. She was completely naked and vulnerable now. Her heart fluttered. They were both naked.

"Keep your eyes averted. Good boy. Now start the shower and remember I like it warm. I will be there shortly." Clara said. She was in charge now. With each tiny instruction, she was slowly conditioning his mind to obey her decisions. His training had begun, and Jacob didn't even know it yet.

Jacob nodded and stared at the ceiling as he stepped around Clara. Once she was out of his field of vision, he looked straight ahead and walked into her beautifully tiled bathroom. Her glass-walled shower stall brought back memories of peeking through the door crack and masturbating while she showered. She could never find out about that little indiscretion. Amazed at his good fortune, Jacob cranked the shower controls and adjusted the water until it was nice and warm.

He then peered towards her bedroom.

"Close your eyes, and keep them closed," Clara said from the other room. She had been watching him.

Fine, Jacob thought with a grin. He stood up and shut his eyes and waited with a smirk on his face. Her little game was turning him on, and he liked it.

Steam from the hot water started to fill the room, adding an aura of mystery. With his eyes closed he imagined Clara appearing out of the mists ready to make sweet love to him, and he could barely contain himself.

When Clara walked into the shower, she slowed to confirm Jacob was following her instructions. She could see his eyes were shut, but he was also sporting a huge erection. Her eyes lingered on it briefly and she nipped her bottom lip with her teeth. She hadn't seen a cock like that for a long time and she felt her heat moisten. Concealed in her hand was a pink vibrator. She quietly placed it on the shower bench. She confirmed he wasn't peeking before letting her eyes admire his muscular young body and hard cock. She was about to teach him a lesson in self-control he won't soon forget.

Stepping into the shower stream, Clara let the warm water wash over her naked body. She shot him a glance. His eyes were still closed. She adjusted the hot water tap a little more to her liking and let the warmth caress her. Jacob had a smirk on his face, and she guessed he might have stolen a peek or two. Not that she minded. Perhaps making him her plaything would prove successful. Oh yes, she thought, he was a play thing. The idea aroused her. She would curb his masturbating addiction and also extract a lot of pleasure from that gorgeous throbbing cock.

"You may open your eyes, but be warned," Clara said in a serious tone, "you may not touch your cock at all. Understood?"

Jacob opened his eyes and focused on her wet body. He nodded and his smirk turned into a handsomely annoying grin. He obeyed and didn't grab his cock. Instead he put hands on hips and regarded her naked body with an appraising eye. Clara watched his expression. She was thirty-four. Would he find her body attractive or repulsive? She hoped what she had to offer pleased his eye. It had been so long since a man of substance even took an interest in her.

She hated that his allure effected her so much. She would have to be strong to resist his masculine charms, especially while being naked and so close to him.

"Now you may stand under the water for a moment, only to get yourself wet. Then take that bar of soap and wash your body thoroughly," Clara said.

She stepped to the side as Jacob approached the water stream, careful to stay out of his reach. He turned his face upwards into the stream and ran his hands through his hair until it was soaked. She liked how it streaked and matted across his brow. Jacob then turned and let the water trail down his back. Clara stole a glance at his impressively hard cock once more. It would soon be hers to enjoy if things went as planned. She could almost imagine it filling her.

Once soaked, Jacob glanced at the bar of soap. Clara nodded. He grabbed the soap and then stepped out of the water stream and stood by the clear glass partition. She resumed her position under the water and watched as he lathered his muscular body. She noticed his thoughtful expression and liked that his wandering eyes traveled up and down her body like she was on display for his enjoyment.

"Close your eyes, and keep them closed," she said, unable to take his gaze any longer. Her mind was running away, and she was losing the will to teach him anything.

Jacob chuckled and shut his eyes as he continued to lather. Under the warmth of the shower, Clara slipped her hand between her thighs. Her pussy was hot and soaked. She bit her lip and focused on his erect cock as her fingers gently stroked her clit. She enjoyed watching him soap himself. He was keeping his eyes closed. That was good. She wasn't sure she could do this with him watching. Well, not yet at least.

When his hand strayed to his erect cock, her interest piqued. She would let him wash his cock, but nothing more. The last thing she wanted was him masturbating in her shower. With his eyes still closed, he lathered his cock and balls and then gave it a few strokes. And then a few more.

"None of that. I said no playing with it." Clara rubbed her clit more rigorously, the power she exerted over him was intoxicating. When his eyes suddenly opened and peered at her, Clara abruptly brought her hands up to shield his view. "Eyes closed, Jacob!"

"Enjoying ourselves?" Jacob asked, peering around her upturned hands.

"Eyes shut!" She moved her hands to block his vision again.

He reluctantly complied and shut his eyes. After giving himself a last defiant stroke he continued washing the rest of his body. "I don't get why I have to shut my eyes for this, and you don't."

"Because I told you. This is part of your punishment and training."

Jacob stopped washing and tilted his head. "Training?"

"No more questions," Clara snapped. She didn't know why he wasn't obeying. She just needed Jacob to shut up for a minute so she could climax. Was that too much to ask? She wanted to punish Jacob, but the idea of training him to be her play thing made her extremely horny and she had to rub one out.

Perhaps she could teach Jacob to please her. She imagined his beautiful mouth on her clit, sucking and licking and she shivered. It was worth a try. She slipped her hands between her legs and rubbed her clit again. Not only was Jacob young and handsome but he was gifted with a gorgeous thick cock and a seemingly insatiable sexual appetite. A man like that can be useful to an older woman–especially if she nurtures and cultivates his skills. She decided once his punishments were over, she would keep him as a long term play toy. She would no longer have to settle on guys like Steve from yoga, or pretend to enjoy the pawing and overused sexual flirtations from older men. She had in her grasp a young man in the prime of his life. He would be hers. She deserved a man like that. She knew Katie would disapprove, so it was crucial that her daughter never find out. Katie was going to dump Jacob, anyway. Until that happened Clara knew she had to tread carefully. Once they were separated, she could then put a protective wing around poor Jacob and console him. Why let this fine young man go to waste? When the time came, Jacob would find her willing to spread her legs for him and offer him a new bed to lay in. Who said Katie was allowed all the fun in the world? It was time for the mom to have some too. None of this would even have happen if Katie had never confessed she wanted to end things with Jacob. Clara just wanted to make sure when her daughter broke up with Jacob, that she was next in line, not a floozy college girl.

"I'm done. Can I rinse now and open my eyes?"

Clara blinked and focused her eyes. *Oh shit.* He was standing covered in a soapy lather and waiting, his gorgeous cock rigid. In her heightened state of arousal, Clara found herself tempted to throw caution to the wind and simply ride his cock. But that wouldn't achieve what she wanted, her mind told her. Riding him now wouldn't teach him a lesson. She had to show restraint.

Clara removed her hand from between her thighs and stepped out of the water stream. "Yes, you may rinse and also open your eyes now. Remember my rules."

Jacob laughed. "Yes, yes. I understand your silly rules."

"Pardon me?" Clara said. Her voice was crisp and firm, like the voice of a mother addressing an obstinate child.

Jacob had stepped under the water and turned to peer at her, his face a little uncertain. "I'm sorry Clara, I mean no disrespect. All these rules just seem silly to me."

She abandoned her wish to jump him right then and there despite how gorgeous he looked. The last thing she could do was reward his poor attitude and ceaseless nattering. He needed so much more training to be a perfect lover.

"You will address me as, Mistress," Clara stated.

"I really have to call you Mistress?" He rinsed the soap from his face and hair, before continuing. "Is that necessary?"

"It is. Don't think I've forgiven you for masturbating young man. You've gone down a notch in my book. You will call me Mistress, and you will earn back my respect. Got it?"

"I got it," he said with a sullen expression. "Mistress."

She could see he was feeling uneasy. As he continued to rinse the soap off his body, his eyes kept glancing at her breasts, or her legs, then back to her breasts. He was horny. His impressive cock never once sagged but stayed rigid and hard. She desperately wanted to feel it inside of her, but she couldn't give in now.

This punishment was supposed to be a learning lesson for him, but Clara was beginning to understand, it was also becoming a learning lesson for her. She would have to remain steadfast and set ground rules. He was an untamed bull, and she was risking a lot being naked with him in the shower. Lesson or no lesson; if he insisted on seducing her in the shower, Clara wasn't certain she could summon the will to fight him off.

"That is enough rinsing. Stand aside," Clara said, glad her voice didn't betray her growing desire for him.

Jacob simply nodded and stepped out of the water stream. He looked her up and down, his eyes sending a thrill through Clara. She suppressed her desires with more effort. His face showed a perpetual smirk that she found difficult to resist.

"You may watch, but no touching me and no touching your cock. I'm serious." Clara grabbed a bottle of shampoo and pouring into her palm. She glanced at Jacob, who seemed intrigued as he watched her.

"You said that already." He folded his arms across his muscular chest feeling amused he was not permitted to touch his cock. He was willing to obey her–for now. It was a fair trade for a free show, he reasoned. But he wasn't going to play her games forever. Sooner or later she would have to give him pleasure or he'd just wait for the opportunity to do it himself.

Carefully lathering her hair, Clara took her time. She enjoyed gazing at his well-muscled body. It was obvious to her that he wanted to start stroking himself. With her hair lathered in shampoo, Clara turned her back towards Jacob, bent slightly, and held her head under the warm water. She had to shut her eyes and work the water through. It was time-consuming but necessary. Men never had to put such effort into their hair washing, she thought.

Jacob glanced at her backside and the curve of her gorgeous ass cheeks. He fought the urge a little longer, then grabbed his cock and started gently stroking. With her back to him and her head under the water, she couldn't see him, so he moved closer and stroked faster. Her glistening backside had trails of shampoo running down it. He watched the soap slide over her ass and trail down her well-formed legs. With his cock mere inches from her wet and glistening ass, Jacob increased his grip and jerked harder still. Showering with Clara, was just too much for Jacob. His desire for her body had been there for so long that he couldn't control his impulses. His face contorted with bliss as his eyes tried to take in every inch of her beautiful wet ass cheeks. His balls convulsed. He suddenly realized he'd gone too far and tried to stop. He gripped his cock in a desperate attempt to force the orgasm back, but it only made it stronger. It was useless. He let out a loud grunt and resumed jerking his cock as his orgasm hit him hard. He shuddered and started spurting hot cum uncontrollably as he jerked and jerked.

Clara stopped rinsing when she heard Jacob grunt. She tilted her head to listen and felt something warm splatter across her ass and lower back. She reached back and felt thick, sticky globs with her fingers. In a panic, she spun around and gasped. Jacob was milking the last drops of his spent cock onto the shower floor. Clara watched in disbelief as his cum mixed with the remnants of her soapy water before circling the drain.

"What the hell did you do?" Clara shrieked as she stepped back. "Did you just cum on me?" She reached both hands behind her back and scooped sperm into her hand then held it up as evidence. "Oh my God you just cummed on me?"

Jacob's face turned crimson, and he looked ashamed. "Was that bad? I didn't mean to get it on you."

"Was that bad? Get out!" Clara shouted. She pointed towards the shower door in a fury, "Just get the hell out right now. That's so disgusting! How dare you!"

Jacob scurried out; his body hunched over and his hands clutching his spent cock. Clara vigorously rubbed her backside under the water. She could feel the spots where his cum had landed. She grabbed her shampoo bottle and hurriedly squeezed a mass into her palm and scrubbed more.

"I can't believe you did that!" Clara accused his retreating form.

He was an untamed bull, Clara fumed. She vowed to make him learn his lesson. And to think she was about to masturbate for him and reward the little twerp by letting him watch. He was nothing but an undisciplined young male interested in only satisfying his cock. Clara felt dirtier than she ever had in her life. She rubbed her backside again with another handful of shampoo. When Clara certain it was all washed off, she carefully stepped wide of the drain. The last thing she wanted was to get it between her toes. She would have to clean the entire bathroom later. Clara slammed the water off and angrily grabbed her towel.

Jacob was standing in her bedroom when she stalked it, a towel wrapped around her body. He was dripping wet, his dark hair a tangle. He stared at the floor like a sullen child waiting to be scolded. She tucked the end of her her towel tighter. The free show was over, and she was pissed.

"What the hell is wrong with you?" Clara said, barely getting the words out.

Jacob shrugged, his face still red. "I'm sorry, I just couldn't help it. I've dreamed about your body so much, and I was so excited I just had to *bust a nut*."

"Bust a nut?" Clara raised an eyebrow. "Is that the term nowadays?" She reminded herself that this man no matter how delicious he looked was still only twenty years old.

"I'm sorry I got it on you."

"You ruined everything I had planned. And to think, you were going to get lucky. But now you've blown it."

"We were going to have sex?"

"Not anymore," Clara said with finality. They weren't, but he didn't need to know that. "Get dressed and leave. I'm sick of your face right now. I'm so pissed off, Jacob, you make me sick. And to think I nearly gave in to you. Get the hell out of here. Grab your shit and change in Katie's room."

Jacob winced. Her words stung. He wanted to say something to make things better but thought better of it and grabbed his folded clothes off the bed.

Clara didn't even watch his muscular backside or admire his cute ass when he left her room to change. She felt dirty and ashamed; dirty because of what he did to her, and ashamed for even getting into the shower with him in the first place. She should have known better. That boy had no self-control. He only thought about himself. Sure she wanted to tease him a little, but with her strict instructions not to touch himself, she thought she could control him. She thought she could cure his masturbating tendencies. But the moment she turned her back, he was back at it, beating off like a retarded monkey.

Toweling herself dry, Clara conceded defeat. If she were determined to punish him, she would have to take more drastic steps. Was it even worth the effort for a guy who can't even learn self-control? She pondered that for a moment. She was furious at him. He did have good qualities, her heart reasoned. Self-control issues aside, Jacob was a handsome young man. He was far better looking than Steve from yoga was, or any man she'd ever been with for that matter. But still, she wondered, was Jacob worth the effort? Would he change? Could he?

An idea popped into her mind, and she pondered it. She needed a way to stop Jacob from jerking off. Something cold turkey. The only way to do that, Clara decided was to use a male chastity device. She knew of a little sex shop about an hour north of town where she could probably pick one up. If not she could order one online. Since he couldn't be trusted not to masturbate, perhaps she could lock his cock away for a while.

The more she considered the idea, the more she was convinced this was her solution. It would be fun, seeing his cock locked up and it would be a lesson in forced self-control. The idea had merit so long as she controlled the key. So long as Clara was the one who decided when his cock was used, she could continue exerting control over Jacob, even when he was home. It would be a twenty-four-hour reminder for him, and an incredible turn on for her.

Throwing on a clean bra and panties, Clara wondered if she had time to make the drive. As she slipped on shorts and a fresh t-shirt, she guessed she could make the drive and be back before supper. Was Katie letting her friends stay one more night? She'd have to check. The more Clara pondered her idea, the more she thought it could work. The fact that her idea would also arouse her had nothing to do with her decision.

Clara tossed her towel in the hamper and folded her arms. She would have to confront Jacob one last time. She had to take control of the situation and show Jacob, who was in charge. She found him in Katie's room using one of her hairbrushes to fix his hair. He stopped and looked up when Clara walked in.

"I'm sorry...Mistress," Jacob said, careful to use the name she wanted. "I don't know what I was thinking. I feel bad. I didn't mean to ruin—"

"Shut up," Clara said.

Jacob clamped his mouth and blinked in surprise. She had never told him to shut up before.

"I've decided that we started off on the wrong foot, so-to-speak," she said in a conciliatory tone.

Hope returned to his face. He put the hairbrush down.

"I should have known better than to bring a young man into the shower with me. I wanted to tease you a little but prevent you from, you know, playing with yourself. I wanted to teach you self-control, and show the benefits to being with a woman, other than jerking off."

"I won't do it again."

Clara raised an eyebrow. "Don't make promises you can't keep. Now, I have a solution to our problem that will allow us to shower together."

Jacob perked up, and his face brightened. Like a man in the desert finding water, he grasped at his chance for redemption.

"You aren't going to like it, though."

His face was undeterred. "Please! Anything," Jacob pleaded. "Just don't tell Katie and don't be mad. I'm really sorry. I love being with you. Honest!"

Holding up her hand, Clara shook her head. "If you accept your punishment and learn your lesson, then there won't be any need to tell my daughter anything."

"Yes, okay."

"Be here tomorrow, at noon. Don't think this is me showing weakness. I'm beyond pissed off at what you did, but I'm willing to try a different approach to rectify our little problem and move on. Part of me, though, thinks you should be out of chances, Jacob. What you did was disgusting and disrespectful. But, in retrospect, I accept partial responsibility for teasing you. Be here at noon tomorrow. This is your last chance."

Jacob nodded, unsure of what she had in mind, but thankful he wasn't going to be banished from seeing her again. He silently vowed not to fuck up again.

"Now go home, Jacob. I really am sick of your face right now."

Understanding perfectly, Jacob ducked out of the room and down the flight of stairs. She heard the front door close and turned to look out the window. From there she watched his retreating form all but run down the driveway and then across to the neighbors house. She wondered why he parked over there. Young men are so irrational, she thought.

Standing at Katie's window, Clara frowned as the realization hit her that she was playing a dangerous game. If Katie found out, she would feel betrayed by her mother. What daughter wouldn't be angry if their mother stole their boyfriend? Was there a way to get Katie's blessing? Probably not. Best her daughter just not know at all. Once they were broken up, Jacob would be fair game.

Feeling somewhat disgusted with herself, Clara got ready to make the drive to the little sex shop. She debated asking Jackie to join her. But then she'd have to explain everything to her friend. Did she want to explain it all? What if Jackie disapproved? It would be a long drive indeed if she had to listen to her friend lecturing her about poor life choices. On the other hand, she really would like to know what Jackie thought. Besides, she doubted Jackie would disapprove of something like this. Heck, Clara thought with a laugh, Jackie would probably want to join in.

"To hell with it," Clara said to a stuffed animal on Katie's shelf. She reached for the phone and dialed Jackie. What are friends for anyway?

* * *

An hour later, Jackie was sitting in Clara's kitchen sipping a lemonade and listening to the whole story.

First, Clara mentioned how Katie and Jacob were on the rocks. Jacob didn't know they were on the rocks; it was just one sided. Katie was thinking about another boy from college–a rich boy that all her friends adored–and had been considering ending things with Jacob for some time now. When Jackie had asked about Jacob, Clara made sure to point out how attractive and handsome he was, while emphasizing his muscular body. She spiced the conversation with comments about his unkempt hair and his ridiculously cute dimpled smile and of course how gorgeous his cock was. Jackie liked that part. She replayed in vivid detail catching Jacob in her upstairs office jerking himself off while watching Katie and her friends lounging around the pool. Clara carefully explained how she planned on punishing Jacob and teach him self-control. Finally, Clara ended by telling Jackie what had just happened in the shower. She laid it all out and felt relieved someone finally knew the whole truth.

"You what?" Jackie's eyes nearly popped out of her head.

"What do you mean by that?" Clara said carefully. She picked up Jackie's empty glass and set it in the sink.

"You got naked with him in the shower?"

Clara nodded innocently, her eyes wide. "Was that bad?"

Jackie shook her head as she shouldered her smart little designer purse and stood up. "Let me get this straight. You showered naked with a horny college guy and are shocked when he jerks off?

"Well, when you put it that way," Clara relented as she grabbed her car keys. "Come on let's drive. We can talk in the car."

Jackie kept shaking her head in amazement as she followed Clara out the front door. If she hadn't known Clara all her life, she would have doubted the story was even true. But hearing it first hand, Jackie knew it was true. Every word of it.

Clara unlocked her convertible. With the beautiful blue sky and an hour of open coastal road each way, she didn't want to be cooped up in Jackie's car.

"You invited him into the shower with you? After you catch him jerking off? In your office? While watching your daughter, topless?" Jackie pulled her sunglasses off the top of her head and slid them on her face. "Are you out of your mind? And you call me the slutty one. Is this story for real?"

"Come on Jackie don't be ridiculous," Clara said defensively. "Of course, it's true. That's why I need your advice on the way to the sex shop."

Jackie laughed. "Why do I get the feeling I just stepped into a porno movie?"

Clara opened the car door and held it open to let the heat escape. She looked across the low-slung roof at Jackie. "When you put it that way, I guess it sounds kind of loopy. I think all boys masturbate; maybe it's like a compulsion. You think I made a mistake?"

Jackie nodded and said, "It sounds farfetched is what I think. So why are we going to a sex shop?"

Unlatching the roof locks, Clara pressed the retract button and watched the convertible top retract. She tossed her purse into the back seat and considered her friend's words. Jackie followed suit and tossed her purse in too.

"You don't know Jacob. He is a nice young man."

Jackie fixed her with a stare. "Apparently not. Nice boys don't spooge all over you in the shower. Also, it's considered rude in polite company to ejaculate on another person without asking. And another thing, I can't understand," Jackie continued, "why are you pursuing a relationship with a guy fifteen years younger than you? My God girl, you're almost thirty-five, and he's not much older than Katie.

Clara slipped into her seat and shut the door. "I don't know if I'd call this pursuing a relationship. It's more of a friend with benefits thing. I just feel like I've spent my whole life raising a kid–who I love with all my heart and don't regret for one minute. I just feel like I missed out on having a guy like Jacob. So what if I have a little crush on Katie's boyfriend? I guess it's just nice to be wanted by someone. That's all. I'm not pursuing a relationship."

"This is totally a relationship." Jackie settled into the car and fastened her seatbelt. "If you want guys who drool over you, then pay attention once or twice in Yoga class. Why are we going to a sex shop? By the way, I have a points card we can use."

Points card? Clara had to laugh at that. "I need a male chastity device," Clara explained and started the car.

"A cock cage?"

"To use the vernacular, yes, a cock cage." Clara backed the car around, doing a half circle and pointing the nose towards the road. Doubt suddenly clouded her thoughts. She put the car in park and looked at Jackie. "Do you think this drive to the sex shop is a bad idea? Should I even bother?"

"You need to have a specific plan before you dive into a relationship with this boy. Let's say you buy this chastity thing. Then what? Are you going to make him wear it all the time or only once in a while? What do you do if Katie finds out? Because Jacob is a male, and prone to being stupid, you have to consider what can go wrong. What do you do if he brags or let's slip that he jerked off in the shower with you?"

"I certainly did not let him jerk off," Clara retorted.

"Katie will think you did and feel betrayed. Imagine Katie's face when she learns you are fucking around with her boyfriend. Can you see that going over well? These are complications you need to consider before going ahead with this plan."

"I see your point," Clara said tapping the steering wheel with her thumbs. "This is getting complicated. But if he mentions the shower, then won't he also have to spill the beans about masturbating while spying on Katie and her friends. I don't think he could bare the humiliation."

"You might be right. All I'm asking is are you willing to take the risk?"

"I think Jacob will keep quiet. He might have a strong libido and no self-control, but I have a feeling he isn't willing to be humiliated. I can use that," Clara said, trying to sound convincing.

"Every man wants to have sex with you, Clara. Just admit this is about being fucked by a younger man, and not about punishment," Jackie said.

"Well he is handsome, but no I can't betray Katie. This isn't about sex."

"You are betraying her already!"

"I don't see it that way," Clara said. She saw it clearly in her mind now. "I am punishing him. I tried to tease him in the shower. That was the wrong approach without first putting his cock on a leash. I see that now. He can't be trusted to follow the honor system so I should have taken precautions. When you think about it, it's his dick that's causing all this drama."

"That's one way to put it," Jackie said dryly. "Dicks have been fucking the world since time began. You can't lock them all up."

"But I can lock this one, and I intend to. Instead of revealing Jacob's indiscretion, I'm dealing with it. If I call the cops, he gets arrested, and his relationship with Katie is over, plus he gets tagged with a criminal record for the rest of his life. It would be his ruin. So in a way, I'm doing him a favor."

"Sounds like you are doing yourself a favor too."

"My idea will work," Clara continued. "I use a cage, and he can't jerk off. Once Jacob's cock is tamed, leashed and completely under my control, I then can train him to show proper restraint. I can do all this without the fear that he will make a disgusting mess. My plan is practically flawless."

"How do you figure that?" Jackie asked.

"Because he won't be able to do the one thing he loves to do. Not without my permission at least. I think Jacob's decisions are based primarily on the desires of his cock, plain and simple. It's time he learned there are consequences and repercussions for his impulses."

"That's settled then. Now, let's take a drive," Jackie said. "I think you have all your bases covered if you're still sure about this course of action."

"I am," Clara said. She felt a weight lifted off her shoulders now that she had vented to Jackie and examined all the angles. She tossed the car in gear. Jackie flipped on the radio and turned it to her favorite station. Clara turned north out of her driveway and stepped on the gas. With the top down and the sun shining along the coastal highway, it didn't take long for both of them to start singing. A few minutes into the drive, Clara turned and peered at Jackie wondering if her friend really did have a points card for a sex shop.

Jackie noticed Clara's gaze and stopped singing. "What?"

Clara just shook her head and kept driving. "Nothing, keep singing."

* * *

Earl Beagle crushed his cigarette in an overflowing ashtray next to the cash register and pulled another from the soft pack in his shirt pocket. Sweat ringed his brow, not from any hard physical work (he abhorred physical work) but from the sweltering humidity in his sex shop. He lit his smoke and took a deep drag before turning his attention once more to his laptop. The air-conditioning was on the fritz. It was on his list of things to do, but he'd get around to it, eventually. Despite the fan spinning at full power, there just wasn't enough air flow to cool the place. Rows of adult DVDs, organized and labeled by genre promised to satisfy just about any sexual taste. Racks of magazines, both current and backdated offered titillating girls and steamy stories. In the back of his store were the private video booths and discrete pump bottles of hand sanitizer and double bagged garbage cans beside ample rolls of paper towel. You weren't permitted to masturbate in the booths, and if you asked, nobody did, but there was no harm in providing lots of sanitizers and towels to customers enjoying the bevy of adult films.

Business was slow, and Earl was tempted to close up his store and head home to the privacy of his basement to work on his current venture. Steve, his business partner, and friend of twenty years had just delivered hidden camera footage from the first ever naked yoga class in San Altra. There were some choice girls.

A car pulled into the parking lot. Earl glanced at the outside camera feed and saw two women step out. He didn't get many women at his store, but that trend was changing the last few years. He thought they were probably tourists but then he leaned closer, and his eyes grew wide. Could it be the two women from yoga? No way he cussed. Had they discovered he had secretly watched and filmed their threesome with Steve? Had they come to confront him?

Snapping his laptop closed, Earl brushed a hand over his thinning hair and cleared his throat. He brushed ashes off the countertop and took a quick drag on his cigarette before extinguishing it in the ashtray. He knew he had mint gum somewhere but couldn't find it.

The door opened, and both women stepped inside the store. Earl masked his astonishment. It was the exact two women he had watched. *Shit!* His heart quickened, and his palms felt suddenly clammy. He decided to see what happens.

"I don't like the smell in here," Clara whispered as she leaned closer to Jackie.

"I forgot to mention he's a smoker, and the place stinks but don't worry," Jackie said quietly. "All sex shops smell like dirty ballsacks."

"Good afternoon, ladies. Anything I can help you with?" Earl asked, making his best impression of someone who cared.

"Just looking for now, thanks!" Jackie replied without bothering to look at him.

Clara turned her head and gave the man a smile which faltered on her face when their eyes met. Something about him struck her as familiar. A moment later her smile faded with recognition. He was the man enjoying a free show when both Clara and Jackie were doing Downward Dog. He was smiling now, and Clara felt a greasy unease wash over her. She turned away and discreetly directed Jackie out of view down the first isle of movies.

Halfway down the aisle, she spun Jackie around and with wide eyes she gripped Jackie's shoulders. "That's the man from the yoga class!"

"What man?" Jackie asked failing to lower her voice.

"Hush, please. Don't look now, but I think that was the guy in the purple tracksuit. Remember him? He was the guy checking out our butts in class? That's him behind the cash register; I'm certain of it."

Jackie crinkled her nose and made a sickening sound. "I remember that guy, and for the record, he was checking out your ass, not mine. You really think that's the same dude?"

Clara nodded.

Jackie frowned. "Fine, stay here." She casually strolled away, glanced towards the man behind the counter and then spun on her heel and quickly returned.

"Well?" Clara asked in a whisper.

"That's him alright. What are the odds, huh?"

"Maybe we should just leave."

Jackie shook her head. "Darling, creepers are all over the place, you can't avoid them. We came here to get stuff for your new pet, and now you're going to turn tail and run just because you run into a pervert?"

Fixing her jaw, Clara nodded. "You're right. Screw him. We'll just get what we came for and go home."

A mischievously dark expression crossed Jackie's face, and Clara hesitated.

"I know that look, Jackie. What are you thinking?"

Jackie tilted her head thoughtfully. "Well, we could mess with him a little. If you don't mind being a little naughty."

"I don't know," Clara said cautiously. "What do you have in mind?"

Jackie winked at her. "Just follow my lead when we go up to pay. First, we need to shop."

Clara chewed her lip. "I hate when you say that."

"You hate to shop?"

"No, I hate it when you tell me to follow your lead."

Jackie giggled and directed Clara to the back of the store where a large array of sex toys, gadgets, lotions and novelty items were on display.

Clara glanced at the choices. "How do I decide?" She absently picked up a restraint bondage kit and flipped the box over in her hands. On the back was a young couple using straps and velcro restraints on a bed. Her mind began to see possibilities with young Jacob.

"I think these are what you're looking for." Jackie pointed at a small rack displaying various sized cock rings and cock cages.

Clara wasn't sure what size of cage she would need and stared at the selection in dismay. She picked a chromed one at random and held it in her hands. "This has weight to it."

Jackie nodded. "I think you'll want something lighter, so your pet can wear it longer. Try to find one made of plastic."

"These are plastic," Clara said. She found a pink one and a naughty smile crossed her face as she thought of Jacob's cock encased in it.

"You'll want to restrain his hands and get a gag too," Jackie suggested. "Trust me, they sometimes talk too much and ruin your fun. I'll get a basket."

Nodding absently, Clara continued to browse, her mind filling with more and more ideas of what she could to do to Jacob. Do people use this stuff? She couldn't help feeling that she had missed out on a lot in life.

When Jackie returned with a basket, Clara dropped in the pink plastic cock cage, a ball gag, the bondage restraint box-set and a blindfold. When she saw Jackie's expression she blushed.

"What?" Clara asked defensively. "I'm just getting the essentials."

"I didn't say anything," Jackie said. "Hey, do you want to watch a porno? They have viewing booths in the back behind those curtains." Jackie pointed towards the red curtain in the far corner.

"No, I'll be fine. Look at my basket and tell me if I'm missing or forgetting anything."

Jackie inspected her items and nodded in approval. "I'd recommend handcuffs and rope. Those are always handy to keep your man from wandering off before you're done with him, you know, while you go freshen up."

Clara giggled. "You sound you know this from experience."

"No comment, but trust me, get the handcuffs," Jackie said. "And rope."

There were all kinds of handcuffs on display. Some had fluffy edges while others gloved in soft velvet. Clara didn't know what to pick. She eventually settled on plain metal cuffs. She held a pair in her hands, then considered for a moment before adding a second pair to her basket–just to be safe.

"Ready?" Jackie asked after dropping a package of soft black rope into the basket.

"I think I am, but I feel nervous buying all this stuff. Jacob won't think I'm a sex freak, will he?" Clara asked.

"Isn't that the point?" Jackie said with an amused grin. "Now listen. When we go up to pay, I'll casually ask you if we have enough sex toys for the orgy."

Clara gasped. "Sex orgy? Jackie no!"

"Trust me," Jackie continued. "Hearing us talk about an orgy will fuck with his mind. Pretend to be nervous and tell him you've never had an orgy before. Then ask if he thinks you bought enough toys for it."

Clara's mouth dropped, and she swatted Jackie's arm. "There's no way in hell I'm saying all that. He's likely to ask where and then show up with a box of condoms. No, it's too gross to even consider."

"But it will be fun," Jackie said. "Come on, Clara, live a little. Live on the edge for once in your life."

"You are such a bad influence on me," Clara said. "What we did with Steve after yoga wasn't living on the edge enough to you?" She pondered Jackie's idea for a minute and then sighed in resignation. "Fine. I have no moral fiber left anyway, so I might as well. Just for the record, we're both going to hell."

"That's the spirit," Jackie said and giggled.

They walked to the counter and Clara placed her basket down.

"Will that be cash or credit?" Earl asked, eyeing the contents of the basket with interest. He picked up a scanner and waited.

"Oh cash for sure," Jackie said. "We don't want our husbands to know we're going to a sex party."

Clara blushed and covered her mouth with the back of her hand. "Yes, this has to stay secret. If our husbands found out we're going to be in an orgy, then geez, imagine all the trouble it'll cause. Heck, they might want to come along."

Jackie nodded and turned to Clara. "Do you think we should get giant rubber cocks? I mean there's going to be what, twenty or thirty guys who'll want to fuck us?"

"Oh, I'd say at least thirty." It was all Clara could do to keep a straight face.

Earl cleared his throat. "Are you ladies planning a party?"

Jackie pretended to be nervous. She fixed the repugnant clerk with her big blue eyes. "It's our first sex orgy, and we'll be the only women there. Maybe you've been to the yoga studio down in San Altra?"

"I've heard of it," Earl said cautiously, eager for more details as he began to scan and bag each item.

"Well, my friend here and I are volunteering to have sex with all the guys who show up. It's a mix between initiation and double dare, and I think someone is filming it too. I'm so excited! I said I could suck off more men than she could, but my friend here disagrees."

"I do," Clara said pointedly. "I'm very good at sucking cocks."

"Filming?" Earl asked, his face turning a shade of red. "When is this party of yours? Maybe I could find guys who are interested in helping you."

"Tomorrow night," Clara said. "I'm kind of nervous. I've only ever had threesomes before now, so I want to be sure I have all the toys and accessories I need to make it through the whole night. Don't tell anyone, please."

Earl acted solemnly and nodded, "Of course not."

"Pinkey swear," Jackie said.

"Not a word," Earl added.

To Clara's surprise, Jackie pulled a wad of cash from her purse and paid for the items. She winked at Earl, which caught him off guard and then turned to leave.

"Best of luck," Earl said. He was clearly processing what they had told him.

Clara beamed like a mindless bimbo. "Well, I best get home and start practicing on those cucumbers. Nice to meet you," she said, following Jackie out the door.

By the time Jackie and Clara were in the car, Earl was already on the phone.

* * *

"Cucumbers? You said cucumbers?" Jackie burst out laughing.

Clara pulled her car onto the highway and hit the throttle. She started to giggle. "I'm sorry, It was all I could think of."

"That poor guy is going to have a heart attack."

Clara shook her head in dismay and tried to control herself. Jackie burst into a fit of hysterics and had to wipe tears from her eyes. "Cucumbers!"

"I will admit that was fun," Clara said a few minutes later.

"You should have seen the look on his face when you said you had to go home and practice. Good god, that was hilarious. Well done."

"I try," Clara said.

They drove the hour back to Clara's house in high spirits. It felt good to laugh, Clara thought as she pulled into the driveway. Laughter and a best friend are all a woman needs in life–well that and a big cock to satisfy her.

"We have to do this more often," Jackie said.

"I agree. Life's too short not to have fun."

"Now you're talking," Jackie agreed. "Let's go inside; I'm dying for a drink. Do you want me to stick around or are you gonna call Jacob?"

Clara climbed out of her car and stretched her legs. "I'll call Jacob and tell him to get his cute little ass over here. In the meantime come inside and have a drink. I think we need to do a little planning on how I'm going to teach Jacob a lesson."

"No, make him come over tomorrow. Let him stew for a while," Jackie said and followed Clara into the house.

"You think I should make him wait until tomorrow? I can do that."

"Are you sure you want my advice on punishing the boy? My mind can go to some pretty weird places," Jackie warned.

Clara smiled. "Why do you think I keep a bottle of the good stuff in the cupboard?"

* * *

The expensive wine paid off in spades for Clara. Not only had Jackie given her a list of suggestions on how best to punish Jacob for his voyeuristic misdeeds, but she also gave Clara a crash course on playing the role of a dominant female. If everything worked as Jackie suggested, then Jacob's selfish focus on pleasuring himself would not only be stopped but probably cured as well.

"So you are certain this will work?" Clara asked. The wine had hit her hard, and she felt her face flush, and her inhibitions weaken. The idea of not only punishing Jacob, but also turning him into something of a fuck toy for her had made her pussy moisten. The games she could play and the frustration she could inflict on Jacob made Clara wonder if she would need another session with pink Pedro.

Jackie drained the last of the wine and set her glass down carefully before speaking. She had played both the role of submissive and dominant and Clara could imagine the dirty sensuous thoughts her friend was thinking.

"Your goal is to do two things," Jackie said. "First of all, you want to show your dominance over this young college boy. He has to learn that you are in charge, and he will be following your rules. He will resist, at first, and maybe try to push the limits, but you must stay strong. Jacob has to learn his proper place in this relationship and learn to obey you."

Clara nodded and played with the last mouthful wine in her glass before downing it. She wondered just how far she could push this whole domination idea. Would Jacob resist? Jackie said he would, and that made sense. No man, especially a young sexually charged man like Jacob, would willingly just give up control of his sex life just because a woman wanted him to. Controlling the cock cage was the crucial key to controlling Jacob.

"Your second goal," Jackie continued as she picked up the empty wine bottle and frowned. "Is to take Jacob's sexual frustration and focus it on pleasing you. Think of it like training a young puppy. The mind of a young man is much the same. He wants something, and you have it. In this case, it's unlocking his cage so he can fuck you and cum. Like a puppy doing tricks for a treat, Jacob will quickly learn he has to please you first to get his cock free. If he fails, then he gets no treats–his cock stays locked up. It's a powerful incentive to learn. Now do you understand the power relationship you're setting up?"

There was another bottle of wine in the cupboard, but Clara decided not to bring it out. She wanted time to process her thoughts, not get drunk with Jackie. She needed to think clearly.

"I think I get it. This key," Clara paused and picked up the small gold colored key and turned it in her hand. "Is crucial in both training and punishing Jacob. Funny how something so small can hold such power."

"That golden key will become his obsession if you do this right. It will unlock a world of pleasure for you as well. Don't forget that. I'm almost envious," Jackie said.

"Well, I'm going to call Jacob and tell him to be here at noon tomorrow. In the meantime, how about a quick dip in the pool?"

Jackie brushed her blonde hair from her face. "I don't have a bathing suit.

"Who said anything about bathing suits?"

Snorting a laugh, Jackie stood. "I knew I liked you for a reason."

* * *

When Jacob pulled into Clara's driveway the next day, he felt a sense of dread. Clara had told him to come over at noon, but then she called again saying she changed her mind and made it two o'clock. When he asked why all Clara would say was her reasons were none of his business. After shutting off his car, Jacob looked at his watch. It was nearly two.

He wondered if Katie and her snobby rich friends were home. They'd stayed since Katie's birthday, and Jacob was more than ready for them to go home. When he asked Clara, she just repeated to be over at two and then hung up on him.

Stepping out of his car, Jacob walked to the front door of Clara's Spanish style home and rang the doorbell. He could have used his key, or simply walked in (providing the door was unlocked) but he decided against it. Something in Clara's tone on the phone told him she was still either very angry or had decided on more punishments. In either case, it probably wasn't a good idea anymore to barge into Clara's home unannounced.

He pressed the doorbell again.

Clara opened the door and stepped back as she swung it wide. She was wearing a black silk bathrobe tied at the waist, a pair of thigh-high stiletto boots, and from the little Jacob could see through the gap in her robe, also a black lace bra. Her long dark hair was pulled back and tied in a tight bun, giving her face the appearance of a strict schoolmaster. Dark mascara and eyeliner made her already beautiful eyes, dark and smokey. Her face had just a touch of foundation and blush, and her lips a deep red hue.

Jacob's jaw dropped, and his eyes became circles. He had never seen Clara dressed like that, and he instantly felt a stir in his pants. All thoughts of repentance vanished from his mind as he soaked in her beauty. Clara wasn't the type of woman who needed makeup to look beautiful. In Jacob's opinion, she was gorgeous just as she was. Her dark mascara, blush, and lipstick only heightened and overwhelmed his senses.

"Come in, Jacob," Clara said in a throaty voice. "I've been expecting you."

Jacob wasn't sure he should go in. She looked so dangerously alluring, and he doubted he would be able to keep his hands off of her. He swallowed hard and stepped inside.

She closed the door, and Jacob heard the unmistakable sound of the deadbolt. Gesturing towards the kitchen, Clara smiled. "Have a seat in here. I have a few things I'd like to show you."

He followed her, his eyes taking in her slim backside and shapely legs as she walked. She turned and pointed to a kitchen stool. Jacob cautiously sat. Laid out on the counter were a variety of kinky-looking sex toys. He felt his heart quicken. He glanced at the toys and then at Clara, with a questioning look on his face. She was looking at him with a faint smile.

"Do you recognize any of this stuff?"

Jacob glanced at the selection once more. Most of the items he did. There was a blindfold, two pairs of handcuffs, a strange plastic device that looked like a hollow penis, a leather crop, two vibrators, a dildo and three coils of soft black nylon rope. He felt his cheeks flush, and he thought Clara certainly had quite the collection of kinky stuff.

"Most of it," Jacob said. "I take it these aren't Katie's?"

"No, these are mine." She picked up the plastic hollow penis and after studying it for a moment handed it to Jacob. "Do you know what that is?"

Jacob didn't, but he could guess it was for him. He stared at it blankly.

"It's a cock cage. For you," Clara said quietly.

"Why do I need this?"

"I've decided you will learn discipline, especially after that stunt you pulled in the shower yesterday. Don't think I've forgotten," Clara said.

Jacob swallowed nervously and watched her set the cock cage on the counter. He glanced over the other toys before looking Clara in the eyes. There was a moment of understanding in the silence that followed. Jacob could see that she intended to play with him while calling it punishment. She was so stunning, and he felt his desire for her grow stronger than ever. Whatever games she wanted to play, he would play them too. Anything just to be close to her was worth it, but this time he was determined not to fuck things up.

"So, this is what will happen," Clara said with firm confidence. "I will assume the role of the dominant, and you will be my submissive. I will try to correct your flaws and turn you into a somewhat presentable man. From now on, I will tell you what to do, what to think, and what to say."

"This is my punishment?" Jacob scoffed. "What if I like it?"

Clara's brows furrowed and her gaze became stern. "Trust me; your cocky tone will change. I will teach you that your cock belongs to me. It's not yours to play with or use without my permission anymore. Furthermore, you will learn basic life skills on how to pleasure a woman. This lesson will serve you well in life, but first, you need to understand our relationship."

Jacob liked the sound of that. "So we are in a relationship? Won't Katie mind? Where is Katie by the way? You never answered me on the phone."

"The first rule you must learn, is not to speak unless asked a question. It is none of your concern where my daughter is, suffice to say she is out with her friends and won't be home until late. From now on, you will only speak when spoken too. Do you understand?"

Jacob rolled his eyes but nodded.

"Don't think I didn't see that," Clara said. She picked up the cock cage and motioned for Jacob to stand. "Take off your shorts."

A grin spread across Jacob's face. Finally, his fantasy of fucking Clara was about to come true. He eagerly jumped up and undid his shorts. He would play her silly girl games once more, but in the end, he would finally have her.

Clara glanced at his erect cock and frowned. "You're hard already?"

Jacob shrugged his shoulders meekly, but the smirk on his face said it all.

She thought for a moment and then said, "Follow me." When Jacob started to bend down and grab his shorts, she wagged a finger. "Leave those. I said follow me, I didn't say get dressed."

Unsure what her plan was, Jacob followed Clara through the living room and the patio doors into the backyard. He paused briefly to make sure Katie and her friends weren't hiding behind the bushes. Perhaps Clara had planned for them to see him naked as a payback. The backyard was empty. His curiosity grew more pronounced, and Jacob gazed at her questionably when Clara stopped and turned. Her black silk bathroom slipped open a little, revealing her lace covered breast. She saw his eye and quickly pulled her bathrobe closed.

"Jump in the pool," she said.

"Pardon?"

"Jump in. The cold water should cool any ideas floating around in your head. Hurry up, I don't have all day," Clara said, folding her arms impatiently.

Pulling his shirt off, Jacob concealed his amusement and dove in. The water was cool, and he felt oddly strange being naked while Clara stood watching him with those smoldering eyes. He doggy paddled around and then changed to a broad stroke reaching the far wall before turning and swimming back.

"Are you soft yet?" Clara asked.

While treading water, Jacob couldn't help but laugh at the ridiculousness of her question. He looked up at her. "Do you want me to check?"

Clara sighed and nodded. "Obviously."

"Nope, still hard," Jacob said in defiance. He was enjoying this.

"Seriously? Fine, swim around but don't come back into the house until that thing has shrunk," Clara said. She walked towards the patio door, but then paused and turned. Jacob was still treading water, his arrogant smile and eyes clearly annoying her. "And that doesn't mean jerking off in my pool either."

Jacob laughed. "I'm offended by that remark!"

"No, you're not," Clara said, and slammed the sliding door behind her.

Back in the kitchen, Clara placed back and forth, her hands on her hips. She felt exasperated. Perhaps training Jacob was going to be a lot more work than she thought. She hadn't expected him to have an erection, but luckily her quick thinking and a cold pool were the perfect solutions.

She had told him not to jerk off in her pool, but would he listen? Clara poured herself a glass of orange juice and drank it all at once. Then she took a deep, calming breath. She felt her forehead with the back of her hand needing to regain her composure. Seeing the lust in Jacob's eyes and then being so close to his naked body was having a reverse effect on her. All her desires from yesterday were flooding back even stronger this time.

Deciding she needed advice, Clara picked up the phone and dialed her friend.

"Hello?" Jackie answered. She sounded sleepy.

"I don't know if I can do this," Clara said.

There was a moment of silence on the other end of the line.

"Okay, what happened?"

Clara brought her friend up to speed on her stymied progress so far. When she finished, she expected to hear sympathy, but instead, Jackie laughed.

"What's so funny?" Clara demanded.

"You are. Do you know how many women our age would die to be in your situation? Think about it, Clara. You have a hot naked guy in your pool who wants to fuck your brains out. Tell me again why you're complaining?"

Clara took a deep breath. "Things just didn't go how I planned them. I wasn't expecting—"

Jacob strode into the kitchen, and Clara looked up. His naked, muscular body, was dripping with water as he smiled at her and waved.

"—Look I have to go." Clara quickly hung up. She glanced at Jacob and then at the water collecting on her floor.

"You didn't give me a towel," Jacob explained. "But on a positive note, my erection is gone!"

Clara glanced at his cock. It seemed the cold water hadn't put much of a damper on this sex drive, but at least he was semi-soft. She could work with that and bit her lip while trying to decide if she should get a towel or cage his cock before it got out of hand again. If Jacob dried himself off with a towel, Clara thought, he was liable to touch himself again, and then she'd be back at square one. While gazing at it, Clara noticed his cock starting to rise. She blinked and then looked at Jacob's face in panic. He was smiling at her that stupid smirk once more painted on his face.

"Not again!" Clara cried. She quickly grabbed the cock cage and rushed towards Jacob. Flashing a disapproving look, Clara quickly knelt on the floor and tried to slip the cage over his rapid growth. It was too late. Just the touch of her hands around his cock sent him into overdrive and Clara sat back on her haunches in despair, a fully erect cock staring her in the face once more.

This whole caging thing wasn't working at all; Clara thought in frustration. She glanced up and felt like slapping the coy smile off his face. All her plans for having fun were on hold because she couldn't do one simple task and contain his erection.

"While you're down there..."

"Oh stop it. You aren't very helpful at all," Clara said taking his offered hand as she got to her feet.

"I did what you asked me," Jacob said in his defense. "Should I go back for another swim?"

"No, don't bother," Clara said in a defeated tone. She tossed the useless cock cage back on the counter and slumped tiredly on a stool.

"I'm sorry," Jacob said.

Clara turned and looked him. He was still dripping water, but his muscular body and tanned skin more than made up for it. She had to admit, his smile was infectious, with those white teeth and those ridiculously handsome dimples.

"I need time to regroup and think of another plan," Clara said. "To be honest, I wasn't expecting this difficulty."

"I'm not trying to be difficult," Jacob said, "But can I have a towel?"

"Upstairs in the bathroom," Clara replied with a wave of her hand. "Careful on the marble, I don't want you to slip."

She watched as he carefully padded out of the kitchen. She felt a stir when her eyes outlined his muscular backside and his firm butt. For some reason, Jacob wasn't acting self-consciously around her, or trying to hide his nakedness. He seemed to enjoy her seeing him naked. Maybe Jackie was right, Clara thought. Maybe I should toss all these toys out and just let him fuck me. The temptation was strong, and they were alone in the house. She couldn't deny how her body responded being near him. She closed her eyes and could almost imagine his strong hands caressing her body and wondered if he was a good kisser.

No.

Clara's mind took over, and she sat upright. She remembered that Jacob had masturbated in her office while looking at her daughter. Then he had the nerve to ejaculate on her back when she was rinsing her hair in the shower. No. That boy needed a lesson, not a reward. The last thing he needed was another girl swooning and fawning over him. Clara decided his flaw wasn't physical–Jacob was an almost perfect specimen of a man–the flaw was in his attitude. He was obviously accustomed to having his way with women, which explained his cockiness. She had to retrain his thinking. She had to make him see that not everything is about his cock. Even if Jacob left her someday (Clara wasn't stupid enough to think he would stay around forever), she could at least make him more appreciative of the women he meets in the future. Perhaps one day some woman somewhere will silently thank Clara for turning Jacob into a perfect man. As noble goals go, it wasn't the greatest, but it wasn't the worst either.

Steeling her resolve, Clara put her hands on the countertop and laced her fingers together. While waiting for Jacob, a grin crossed her face as an idea came to her. When Jacob came downstairs, he would find a very different woman waiting for him.

Jacob returned a few minutes later and stopped in the middle of the kitchen. He placed his hands on his bare hips knowing his cock hung fully within her view.

"I'm all dried off, Mistress. Am I permitted to clothe myself now?"

Clara purposely avoided looking at his package. Instead, she scooped the handcuffs and nylon ropes in one hand and a tea towel in the other and then stood. "Grab one of those kitchen chairs and follow me."

With an amused eyebrow, he examined the cuffs in her hand. He then sauntered over to the kitchen table and pulled out one of the solidly built wooden chairs. He lifted it easily and followed Clara into the living room. He had no idea what she had in mind, but he was eager to find out.

"Set it here, facing the couch," Clara said, indicating a spot on the floor. When he had complied, she carefully laid the tea towel across the cushioned seat and stepped back. "Sit down, hands behind the chair."

"I just want to warn you, Clara, that I find handcuffs a big turn on," Jacob said. When Clara failed to take his bait, he shrugged and sat. Reaching behind the wooden back of the chair, he clasped his hands together and waited. He felt the cold metal handcuffs around his wrists as she cinched the cuffs tight. Picking up one of the coils of soft black rope she secured his ankles to the chair legs. Finally, she took the last coil of rope and wrapped it around and around Jacob's torso before tying the ends to the back of the chair. Double checking her knots and the cuffs, Clara was satisfied. She stood and stepped back, thinking she didn't do too badly for her first time binding someone to a chair.

"Can you move your arms? Is the rope too tight?"

Jacob tugged on the cuffs. He then tried to flex his legs and finally his chest. He had never experienced bondage, and though he was restricted, he liked where things were going. "It's snug, but I'll manage."

"Good because I don't want you touching me during what comes next," Clara said. She walked a slow circle, tracing a finger across his bare muscular shoulders and back, and then up his neck and across his angular jawline. Jacob smiled and gave her a masculine demonstration of how helpless he was by straining against his bindings. Her eyes widened. She liked how ferocious he was. It turned her on.

Standing in front of him, Clara faced Jacob. From the chair, he peered into her eyes and grinned as she stared intently back into his. For a moment neither of them spoke or moved. Her hands slowly reached to open her bathrobe and Jacob's eye flickered briefly. Suppressing a grin, Clara opened her silk coverings and let it slide off her shoulders. She was wearing a lacy black bra that highlighted her deep cleavage and matching thong panties that showed off her backside. Her thigh-high stiletto boots were a gift from her friend Robin who didn't want them anymore, and she thought they gave her lingerie a nice touch of dominance.

Jacob tore his gaze from her eyes and stared hungrily at her body. She could almost feel his desire traveling from her face to the tips of her stiletto boots and back up again. His cock responded to what his eyes were seeing, and it throbbed helplessly, his cuffed hands unable to stroke it.

"Do you like my little outfit?" Clara asked. She enjoyed knowing he couldn't touch her as she posed for him. She turned first one way and then the other, offering him different profiles before giving him a complete twirl.

"I'm stunned," Jacob croaked, and then cleared his throat. "I don't think that's the outfit you should have worn if you were trying to get rid of my erection."

"I decided not to fight it," Clara confessed in a naughty tone. When Jacob seemed confused, she tilted her head thoughtfully. "What's the matter?"

"I have a confession to make," Jacob said.

"Another one?"

"I was never going to mention this, but since I'm tied up and we're about to have sex, I think I should mention something."

"Go on," Clara said folding her arms. "I'm listening."

"I have a crush on you." His cheeks flushed, and he looked away.

Clara giggled in spite of herself. "Oh do you? I couldn't tell."

"Yes," Jacob said. Gathering his courage, he turned to look in her eyes. His gaze was fierce, and it gave her pause. "I've had one since the first time I saw you. I know I'm dating your daughter, but in my heart, I wish I was dating you. I know it's stupid, but there, I finally said it. It's out."

"I suspected you did," Clara said.

"You did?"

"Come now, Jacob, don't play stupid. It's not very becoming."

Jacob shook his head. "Do you... I mean, is there a chance—"

"That I feel the same about you?" Clara interrupted.

Jacob nodded his eyes filled with hope.

"That depends on you," Clara said as she mused. "I expect a man to act a certain way and show some respect to a woman. Perhaps after I've trained you a little, we'll see. What I want is a man who obeys me. So far you've done anything but that."

"I'll do anything you want," Jacob promised.

Clara laughed. "Young man, hasn't anyone ever told you? Don't make promises you can't keep."

"Please," Jacob said. "I'm begging you. Train me. I'll be good, I promise."

As if considering his words, Clara reached behind her back and unclasped her bra. Jacob's eyes became hungry saucers, and he strained against his bindings. She smiled and carefully brought the straps forward, slipping her arms through the loops. While keeping her breasts covered with her arms, she dropped the bra.

"Is there something you want?" Clara asked in an innocent tone.

Jacob nodded.

"You want to see my bare breasts don't you?"

"Yes I do, please," Jacob whispered, his eyes willing her arms to drop.

"You've been dreaming of seeing these breasts, haven't you?"

Jacob nodded.

Feeling herself get moist, Clara lowered her arms exposing her bare breasts. She brought her hands up and seductively caressed the sides of each breast then squeezed them together and massaged them.

"Or maybe you want to see my bum?" Clara asked as she giggled and hooked her thumbs into her lace panties and wiggled them off. "Is this what you'd rather see?"

Jacob moaned and leaned forward pulling the ropes around his chest taunt.

"Which part of my body did you fantasize about the most?" Clara asked, "My breasts or my ass?"

Jacob was at a loss for words.

"Answer me, or the show is over," Clara said. She turned to give Jacob a brief view of her ass before facing him once more and giving her breasts a wiggle.

"Both... I don't know," Jacob confessed.

"Decide," Clara demanded. "Which one?"

He squinted his eyes to think for a moment. His thoughts were muddled. "I've dreamt of your breasts and also your ass. So both I guess?"

Clara leaned forward thrusting her breasts Jacob's face, but stopping an inch from his straining mouth. She rubbed her hands over each breast and then milked and squeezed her nipples while enjoying Jacob's struggled to reach one with his mouth. Dropping her hands and grasping his erect cock, Clara squeezed. Jacob gasped and held very still his eyes wide with shock.

"Let's get one thing straight. You don't fuck my tits, or do me up the ass or satisfy any one of those juvenile urges running through your head. Do you understand? I decide what happens. Not you."

Jacob nodded, his wide eyes filling with understanding.

"This cock," Clara paused to tug harder, "belongs to me now. You don't play with it unless I tell you to. Is that clear?"

Apprehension filled his face for the first time as Jacob nodded.

"Tell me I own your cock."

Jacob pursed his lips.

"Tell me now!" Clara said, her hand gripping his cock even harder.

Jacob swallowed. "You do?"

"Your words don't sound very convincing." Clara released her grip and stepped back. She regarded Jacob with a look of disgust. "I want you to know I'm only interested in a man who is willing to give up control of his cock to me. Maybe we should stop now."

"No, please! I just needed some time to understand," Jacob cried.

Folding her arms, and covering her breasts, Clara began to tap her foot. "Convince me."

"My cock is yours," Jacob promised with all the sincerity he could muster. When he didn't see her expression soften, he pressed on. "I won't touch it without your permission, I promise."

Clara smiled. "Is that a promise you can keep? Because if it is, we can continue with this relationship."

"It's yours, I swear. Do anything you want with it. Please!"

"Very well then," Clara conceded. He was clearly rattled. She leaned closer, giving him an ample view of her bare breasts once more. "You see how much better things are when you follow my rules? You may suck one breast, but make me believe you want it, or else I take it away."

Jacob's face melted with relief as he eagerly opened his mouth.

Clara plopped her breast into his waiting mouth and closed her eyes, enjoying the pleasure that coursed through her naked body. His mouth was warm and eager as he lapped and sucked her offered breast. Clara felt a tiny tremor in her pussy and sucked in her breath through clenched teeth. No one had ever devoted so much passion and tenderness to a part of her body before.

After a moment, Clara pulled back. Her breast made a popping sound as Jacob's mouth broke away. Her nipple was hard and erect and she caressed and plucked it. Jacob strained for more until Clara calmly switched sides and plopped her other breast into his mouth. More sensations caressed her body and Clara suppressed a shudder. She couldn't recall her breasts ever being so sensitive and could barely contain herself.

"That's enough." She abruptly stepped back, her face flush.

Jacob groaned, his cock throbbing with arousal. "Please, more."

"The second rule I will teach you today, is that your purpose is to give me pleasure, not yourself. It doesn't matter how little or how much pleasure I allow you to have; you will *never* beg for more. Your only concern is *my* pleasure. The needs and desires of that cock are not important."

Jacob nodded and sullenly closed his mouth.

"Time to recap. What's the first rule?"

Jacob pondered for a second and then looked up. "You own my cock?"

"Very good," Clara said patting his cheek. "And the second?"

"My only purpose is to please you, and I should never beg?"

"See, I knew you were more than just a gorgeous cock," Clara said.

Jacob beamed at the compliment.

Reclining on the couch, Clara smiled seductively. Jacob strained against his bindings as he watched her, wondering when she was going to give his cock some much needed attention. She slowly spread her legs and revealed her aroused and swollen pussy lips. His eyes focused like hungry dogs straining at the leash, but he did not beg, though his face contorted with longing.

"Oh my! Look how wet I am," Clara exclaimed like an innocent school girl. She giggled nervously and caressed the sides of her clit, up and down, and then slipped a finger inside. She closed her eyes and moaned.

Straining once more against the ropes that held him in the chair, Jacob did a series of hip thrusts as if his cock was plunging into her wet and swollen pussy. His cock started oozing pre-cum. Clara savored his flustered expression while she played with her pussy. If she weren't careful, she would have an orgasm any moment. Maybe she would. He could wait.

"Remember your purpose," Clara said, taunting him further by squeezing her breast. "All that matters is that I am satisfied, not you. Your cock doesn't interest me right now, so you'll just have to wait while I enjoy fingering myself."

Jacob moaned, his face flushed with desire. He thrust his hips in one last act of defiance before slumping in the chair. Helplessly, his lust filled eyes watched as Clara continued to rub her clit.

"Tell me what you would do if you were untied and could have your way with me?" Clara asked. She gazed at his neglected aching cock and continued to masturbate, content in knowing how much he was suffering strapped to the chair.

Jacob cleared his throat and had to force his brain to think. "Well, first of all, I would kiss you."

Clara moaned. "I'd like that. Where would you kiss me?"

"All over your body, but I'd start with your lips. Then I would kiss softly down your neck and all over each gorgeous breast."

"I like that, keep going," Clara said. She felt her pussy respond to Jacob's images in her mind. It would be nice to have a man kiss her all over.

"Then I would suck your breasts and nibble each nipple until they were hard and erect. After that, I would kiss my way down to your belly button and do a tiny circle."

Clara gasped and rubbed her clit a little quicker. "Tell me more."

Jacob began to speak faster. He could see the effect his words were having, and it excited him. "Next, I would spread your delicious legs and lick your pussy. I would tease you at first, but then I could latch onto your clit with my mouth and suck on it. I wouldn't stop until you had an orgasm."

Clara began to breathe harder, and her hand moved quicker. She turned her head and scrunched her nose as a tiny whimper escaped her lips. "Yeah? Then what?"

"I would make you kneel on the ground and open your mouth," Jacob said. He glanced at his neglected throbbing cock and strained against the cuffs in a desperate need to stroke it. "Then I would force you to suck my hard throbbing cock, back and forth until I was about to cum."

Clara bit her lip and began to rub furiously now. "I'd like that."

"You'd like to suck my cock?"

"Oh yeah, more than anything. Keep going!"

"Then I would bend you over that couch and ram my cock into your hot tight pussy, and I would grab your hips, and I would thrust in and out as hard as I could, not caring that you were having an orgasm. I would keep going in and out until I couldn't hold it anymore. Then I would slam it all the way in and I would cum hard deep inside you."

Clara shuddered and brought her knees together, her legs quivering in a spasm. She gasped, and a strained cry escaped her lips. She extended her legs and locked them; her shapely calves and thighs taunt as an orgasm washed over her. She slowed her probing fingers letting a second orgasm flutter and crest through her abdomen as he legs twitched. Opening her mouth, she drew in gulps of air, and her face flushed deeply. She slowed her hand as her orgasm faded until it eventually stopped leaving a contented afterglow. She was still for a moment, savoring the experience and then opened her eyes. A deep sigh escaped her lips as Clara smiled contently.

"Wow, I needed that," Clara confessed with a giggle.

Jacob wanted to beg Clara to let him cum, but he remembered the second rule. He closed his eyes as his mind replayed what had just happened. His aching cock begged to be touched and oozed slippery pre-cum. He thought if he didn't cum soon, he was going to explode. His arousal was so strong he feared the slightest touch would trigger an orgasm. When he opened his eyes again, Clara was watching him.

"Would you like to cum?"

Jacob nodded in desperation.

Clara scurried off the couch and knelt on the floor between his legs. She grabbed his cock and gave him a couple of strokes. His cock responded by flooding his body with pleasure and his balls twitched, he was that close to orgasm. He moaned.

"Would you like to cum in my mouth?"

Jacob couldn't believe his ears and looked down with a surprised expression.

"No," Clara said as if reconsidering. "I don't think you deserve that. I got what I wanted, so why should I satisfy you?"

"Please," Jacob begged, ignoring the second rule. "I want to cum."

"I think you've done that enough these last few days," Clara observed. "Maybe it's time you didn't have an orgasm for once."

Jacob eyes flashed in frustration. "Please, I'll do anything. You can't just tease me like this."

"Oh but I can," Clara said. "Tell you what. Since there isn't anything in this for me, how about I make you an offer?"

"Anything, Clara. I have to cum."

"I will stroke you off, but afterward, you have to promise to wear the cock cage until our next session. Let's say in two days. Is that a deal?"

Jacob tried to think, but he was overwhelmed with the desire to blow his load. He nodded and accepted her offer. At that moment he didn't care what condition Clara made. All he needed right now was some release, and he'd do anything to get it.

"Very well, you may cum," Clara said with amusement. She started to stroke his impressive cock while massaging his balls. It took all of her willpower not to forgo the hand job and simply mount him. She guessed she might get at least one more orgasm before poor Jacob's cock erupted inside of her. Did she want him cumming inside of her? She had to stay focused, though, so she clenched her legs together and continued to stroke him.

"I bet you want to cum all over my face don't you?"

Jacob cried in desperation, silently mouthing the word *faster*.

"Let me know when you're close," Clara ordered and stroked faster careful to keep a steady rhythm.

She could tell he wasn't going to last. Perhaps another minute of stroking and Jacob would orgasm. Just as she expected, twenty seconds later, Jacob sucked in his breath and nodded frantically.

"Ready to cum all over my face?" Clara asked, stroking with more purpose.

"Yes... oh god, here it comes!" Jacob cried.

Clara waited until the last possible moment, then abruptly released his cock and sat back. "I changed my mind."

"What?" Jacob gasped, just as he began to spurt. He squirmed and struggled as his cock, now out of her hand, throbbed and sputtered aimlessly.

"I changed my mind," Clara repeated with a wicked grin. The sexual torment on his face was clearly evident, and she enjoyed seeing him squirm.

"Please, oh please stroke it. Rub it. Please hurry!" Jacob begged as his orgasm spilled out.

Clara leaned back and rested against the couch watching in fascination as his ruined orgasm faltered and fizzled. She was amazed at how much cum his balls kept pumping. It dribbled and spurted uselessly down the sides of his cock like a shaken soda bottle suddenly opened.

"What made you think I'd want all of that on my face?" Clara asked when his orgasm had sputtered to a messy end.

Jacob rolled his head and whined.

"That, my darling, is called a ruined orgasm. Get used to them because you'll be getting a lot more," Clara said while getting to her feet.

"Why? Why did you do that?" Jacob asked in a quiet voice.

"Because it amuses me to watch you squirm. Now, I believe we had a deal. I'll be right back," Clara said and went to the kitchen to fetch the cock cage.

When she returned, Jacob was pouting. "You tricked me."

"No I didn't," Clara said as she knelt once more in front of his chair.

"You said I could cum on your face," Jacob stated, his eyes hurt.

Clara chuckled. "And I changed my mind. Now, how am I supposed to put your cock cage on when you made such a mess? You see, Jacob, this is why men should very rarely be allowed to blow their loads. Men always make such horrible, disgusting messes."

Jacob looked down and winced. His stomach and chest got the first cum shots, but the rest had dribbled into his lap. His cheeks burned with humiliation. Never in his life had he ever experienced a ruined orgasm, and he wasn't sure he liked it.

"Stay here," Clara said. She put the cock cage down and went back to the kitchen to get a wet washcloth. Returning moments later, and still naked, she bent over and scrubbed his mess. She didn't mind that he was glancing at her dangling swaying breasts. He was bound tightly and wouldn't be touching them.

"Thank you," Jacob said.

Clara was startled and folded the soiled cloth over on itself. "What for?"

"For cleaning me up, and for everything, I guess."

Clara glanced at his face. This must be one of those honest moments men have after sex, she thought. She had read about this.

"You're welcome," Clara said. She ruffled his hair before returning to the kitchen and tossing the soiled cloth in the garbage. When she returned to the living room, Jacob craned his neck and looked at her.

"Honestly, I mean it. I had no idea you were such a cool lady."

Clara rolled her eyes. "First of all, never call me *lady* again. You make me feel old. Now hold still, I've never put one of these cock cages on a man before."

"Will it hurt?"

"How should I know?" Clara said. "If it helps, I read the package, and it says you can comfortably wear it for prolonged periods of time. See that little opening in the tip?" Clara held the plastic cock cage closer to his eyes and Jacob peered at it. "Well, that's for taking a leak. The sides have little openings too so your poor cock can breathe without getting all sweaty. I'd probably suggest using a mild shampoo down there."

"Why do I have to wear it and for how long?" Jacob asked. He was getting a little nervous about having his cock clamped inside the device.

"Really? Haven't you figured it out yet? You have to wear it because you haven't earned my trust. You jerked off looking at my daughter, and you made a mess in the shower. We just went over all of this. I'm *never* going to turn you into a proper young man if you keep ejaculating all the time. As for how long?" Clara considered that for a moment. "Like I said, we'll try two days for now and see how it goes."

"Two days without a hard on?"

"*Hardon* is such a tacky word, but yes, no pardon or blowing your load for two days." She said and then added, in a very calm voice, "If you complain, I can easily add on more days if you'd like."

Jacob shivered and quickly shook his head. He watched as Clara slipped his balls and soft cock through the plastic ring and then held the ring against his abdomen. Next, she inserted his cock into the cage and lined up the connecting pegs before snapping the retainer clips in place. Lastly, she dangled a tiny golden lock in front of Jacob's eyes. She slipped the lock through the reinforced clasp clicking it in place with finality. To test how secure the cage held, Clara tugged, and Jacob winced.

"I think that looks about right," Clara said. "How does it feel?"

"Weird," Jacob replied. "I've never worn anything like this before."

"That's because no woman has ever decided to train you properly. Now, before I forget, I need to hide this key somewhere."

With a forlorn expression, Jacob watched Clara leave the room to hide the key. When she was gone, he looked at his caged cock with an apprehension bordering on panic. He now wondered about the wisdom of giving control to her, but when he considered what he would be getting in return–sex with Clara eventually–the price didn't seem too steep. Jacob reminded himself what the prize was. He could go two days without relief for a chance to fuck Clara.

When Clara returned, the key was gone, and she was carrying a roll of paper towels. Bending down, she unlocked his cuffs and removed the ropes. Jacob was surprised that she was unlocking him and guess his play time for the day was over.

"Stand up," Clara said.

Jacob stood.

"Walk around a little. I want to make sure it fits properly and doesn't pinch. I took the liberty of hiding the key, so don't bother trying to find it."

"I would never do that," Jacob replied in jest. He walked towards the kitchen and then turned and walked back. "I think it fits. It's lighter than I thought I would be."

"Good," Clara said and tossed him the roll of paper towel. "Clean up the rest of your mess and put the chair away. Then meet me in the shower upstairs, I think it's time to continue where we left off yesterday. I'm not quite done with you yet."

Jacob waited as Clara deftly scooped the ropes and cuffs and strode out of the room leaving him alone. His eyes couldn't help but follow her backside. He never got tired of seeing her beautiful ass cheeks jiggle as she walked. He yanked a stretch of towel off the roll and wiped up the chair. The tea towel was stained and needed washing, so he scrunched it into a ball.

He'd bring it upstairs and toss it in her hamper before joining her in the shower. A grin crossed his face as he finished up. If she thinks a silly little plastic device was going to stop him from having fun, he thought, then Clara was in for a big surprise.

Setting the paper towel on the kitchen counter, he tossed the used portion in the garbage. Clara would be waiting for him in her bedroom, and he savored the prospect of joining her. But she could wait. First, he needed a drink. He opened the cupboard, grabbed a glass and ran some cold water. Finishing the first cup quickly, he refilled it and downed another. Being tied up was thirsty work he chuckled to himself as he set the empty glass in the sink.

While whistling to himself, Jacob strode towards the marble staircase. The front door unlocked from the outside. Just before reaching the stairs, he stopped and looked up in surprise as the front door suddenly opened wide, revealing Katie and her friends, arms filled with shopping bags, lattes, and cell phones.

Katie and her girlfriends stopped in the doorway, all eyes turning at once to take in the sight of Jacob standing naked except for a cock cage. Unable to think or move, Jacob remained frozen. He did the only thing that came to his mind and waved his hand with a cheery, "Hello."

Katie blinked with incomprehension for a moment. And then she screamed.

Clara was in her bedroom neatly folding her silk robe when she heard her daughter's cry. She whipped her head around, her only thought was the realization that Katie was home, and Jacob was still downstairs.

"Oh, no," she gasped, dropping her silk robe.

In a flash, Clara grabbed a more sensible bathrobe, throwing it on while she dashed out of her bedroom sprinting for the stairs. Grabbing the banister, she flew down the steps two at a time but stopped at the halfway point. It was too late. Jacob still hadn't moved. He was staring at Katie in shock just as much as she was staring at him. Behind Katie, her girlfriends recovered from their surprise and started laughing at Jacob. Someone held up a phone and snapped a picture.

"Out!" Clara bellowed. Everyone's eyes turned towards her. She descended the remaining steps, her arms waving. "Everyone out except you Katie. Please just back up." Clara reached the front door and forced it closed.

"Mom? Katie asked in a shocked, disbelieving voice. Why is Jacob naked in our house with you? And what is that around his penis?"

One of the girls peered through the front window. Clara cursed and wrung the curtains closed. When she turned and saw the shattered look on Katie's face, she felt like the worst mother in the world.

"Please, let's go upstairs. I can explain everything."

Katie recovered her senses and shook her head. "I don't think I want to go upstairs, mom. What were you doing my boyfriend?"

"Katie," Jacob implored, after finding his voice. "Listen to Clara, please."

Katie backed away and pointed at Jacob. "You just stay the hell away from me. I don't know what kind of freaky shit is going on here, but we're done. It's over."

Clara stepped between them and placed her hands on Katie's shoulders. "Look at me." When Katie didn't look at her, she shook her shoulders gently. "Look at me, I said. Let's go upstairs, honeybun, I think we need to talk."

Katie finally looked at her mother. When she did, her face contorted as tears welled in her eyes. "Fine, but there better be a damn good reason why my boyfriend is naked alone in the house with you."

She broke Clara's hold and stormed up the stairs. Clara sighed and gestured for Jacob to follow. A fine mess she created, Clara thought in despair. What was she going to tell her daughter? A range of ideas flowed through her mind. Honesty would be the best course of action, but not too much honesty. There was no need to confess to Katie that she thought Jacob was a hot stud, and only a fool would dump a boy like that. Clara knew that it was always possible that Katie would find out. It was a risk she was willing to take, and now she had to face the music.

Katie had stormed into her pink themed bedroom and was sitting on her pink bed, arms folded with a scornful look on her face. Jacob wisely snatched a towel from the bathroom and wrapped it around himself to cover his nudity.

When Clara walked into Katie's room, she glanced at Jacob, who was tucking in his towel and trying to look invisible. She leaned against the doorframe and settled her eyes on her distraught daughter sitting on the bed. This wasn't going to be easy, she thought, but she had, to be honest with her daughter.

"Why was Jacob naked and what is that thing he was wearing?" Katie asked.

"Before I answer that, I need to explain a few things first."

"Fine. Explain then."

Jacob tried to blend into the walls.

"Remember when you and your girlfriends had a little swim in the pool?" Clara asked. She could see Jacob tense, but there was no other way around this. Katie had to be told the truth. It was the only way she could think of to explain why Jacob was practically naked.

Katie glanced towards Jacob and then back at her mother. "What about it?"

"I discovered Jacob up in my office," Clara paused trying to decide the most diplomatic way of continuing. "He was stimulating himself."

"He was what? What do you mean?" Katie asked, her face confused.

Clara sighed and came right out with it. "I caught Jacob masturbating."

Katie's head snapped back in shock. "He was jerking off in your office?"

"While looking out the window that overlooks the pool. Remember when you and your friends took your tops off?"

Katie nodded.

"He saw everything," Clara stated.

"He was spying on us?" Katie asked. Her cheeks flushed with anger. She turned and glared at Jacob. "Is this true?"

Jacob nodded.

"Why? Why would you do something like that?"

Looking away, Jacob couldn't answer. *Because they were topless, and he thought he could get away with it.* But he said nothing.

"That doesn't explain what I saw five minutes ago," Katie said.

"I'll explain in a minute," Clara said in a soothing voice.

"No, mom, I want to know right now."

"I said I'll explain in a minute, dearest," Clara said in a firmer tone. When it was clear to her that Katie would listen, she continued. "I didn't want to make a ruckus out of it, so I told Jacob at the time that I would deal with what he'd done later. You may think I used poor judgment, dear, but that was what I decided at the time."

Katie was not convinced. "So having my boyfriend strut around practically naked was your way of *dealing with it later*?"

Jacob shrank further into the wall.

"Not exactly. I knew you were talking about breaking up with Jacob, and I knew if I said anything about what I found him doing, then your relationship would surely have been over," Clara explained. "I thought I was helping."

"You were going to dump me?" Jacob asked, looking at Katie.

Both women pierced him with glares, and he clammed up.

"I told you I was only thinking about it, mom. Thanks for spilling the beans."

"And I had advised against it," Clara countered. "I knew if you discovered what he had been doing up in my office, then you would surely break up, so I decided to take matters into my hands. This is my house you know. I am allowed to handle things the way I see fit."

Katie rolled her eyes.

"The reason you saw him wearing that device was that I had bought it for him. It's a cage, and it prevents a male from achieving an erection. I thought if I caged the problem, then he would suffer for a while and maybe learn something about appropriate behavior."

Blinking in confusion, Katie looked at Jacob. "A what?"

"She bought me a cock cage," Jacob explained, opening his towel and revealing his locked cock. "So I wouldn't be tempted to masturbate around you anymore." His cheeks turned bright red.

Katie's anger was momentarily set aside as her curiosity took over. She peered closely at the device around his cock and realized it was the first time she had seen it. After realizing what she was staring at, Katie quickly averted her eyes. "I had no idea there were such things. Does it work?"

"We don't know," Clara replied. "Cover yourself Jacob. He had just put it on when you got home *early*."

"And where were you?" Katie asked turning towards her mom with an accusing eye. "You guys weren't fooling around were you?"

"Katie," Clara said in dignified outrage. "Do you think so little of me?"

"We didn't do anything," Jacob said. "In fact, she was upstairs the entire time."

Katie glanced at Jacob and then at his towel. She seemed to be considering something. "You jerked off while watching my friends and me in the pool?"

Jacob nodded in shame. He would never have guessed you could have the best time of your life, and the worst, both on the same day.

"I appreciate what you are trying to do," Katie said in a more conciliatory tone looking back at Clara. "But what he did is unforgivable. I don't care that you were trying to help. It's over between Jacob and me."

"No," Clara gasped. "You're making a big mistake. He can be fixed."

Jacob's face contorted, and his eyes brimmed as anguish filled him. He shook his head and looked away. "So it's over?"

"I wasn't going to tell you this, but I've met another guy at school."

"You have?" Jacob looked up.

"He's very rich, and he's very nice," Katie said matter-of-factly. "He wanted to date me, but I was faithful to you, but now I see that was a mistake. It's over between us Jacob. Goodbye." Katie turned towards her mother. "You can have him."

"Katie, you are making a big mistake here. Jacob is a good catch. Don't throw him away just like that," Clara said.

But Katie wasn't listening. She got up and with a haughty toss of her blonde hair, strode out of her bedroom. She abruptly stopped in the hallway as if deciding something and then came back. She stood placing hands on hips and looked at Jacob and Clara like she was going to make an announcement.

"What?" Clara asked.

"So that you know, *mother*," Katie said in an accusing voice. "I found a pair of *your* panties in *my* garbage can covered in *his* sperm."

Jacob tensed and cursed silently. He'd forgotten about that. He had tossed the panties in the garbage on Katie's birthday, after using them as tissue while he jerked off watching Katie's mom. *Shit shit shit.*

Clara blinked in surprise and turned towards Jacob.

"So don't think I didn't know you two were fucking," Katie added. She stomped over to her trash can and rummaged through it. A moment later she yanked the evidence out and held it triumphantly for all to see.

Clara gasped in confusion. "How did..?"

"We didn't have sex," Jacob confessed, his face a mask of despair.

Both Katie and Clara looked at him.

"The day of your birthday party I came over to help decorate, but I dozed off. I woke when your mom got home, and I panicked and never said anything, so she didn't even know I was here. I thought she might be mad that I was in the house uninvited. While trying to figure out what to do, I heard her getting into the shower. I was curious and spied on her—"

"You what?" Clara's eyes were daggers.

"I spied on you in the shower, and then I... you know... sort of soiled your panties because I didn't have any tissues. I wasn't expecting to do what I did, but they were all I could find. I didn't want to make a mess on your floor. I'm sorry."

Katie dropped the panties in disgust, and they fell back into the bin. "You are a disgusting person, Jacob. So not only did you spy on my friends and me, but you also spied on my mom too? I'm so outta here. You can have him, mom."

Jacob reached out to explain, but Katie brushed his arm aside and stormed out of the bedroom. When she was gone, his gaze turned towards Clara. She was staring at him with disgust on her face. He lowered his eyes and studied his feet.

"I don't know what to say," Clara said. "You spied on me too? How many times? What *else* don't I know about?"

"Just once," Jacob told his feet. "I'm sorry. Look all I've ever wanted from the beginning was you. I knew I couldn't have you or be with you or touch you. You consume my thoughts. It was wrong to spy on you like that, but I had to. I couldn't take the torment anymore."

"You sure chose a strange way of showing it," Clara said. She didn't know what else to say. She felt violated but also turned on. It was a strange mixture of emotions.

"So is all this over? Should I go home?" Jacob asked. "I don't care about dating your daughter. Just between you and me, Katie was a horrible girlfriend. From the start all I've wanted was you. What happens to us?"

In a way, what he said was cute and adorable, but also horribly gross and violating. He had covered for her, by lying to Katie. He could easily have confessed everything, but he didn't. Katie would have lost her mind over that. So it appeared there was enough blame to go around. She could point fingers at Jacob for inappropriate behavior, but he could just as easily point right back.

Clara had to admit that Katie never was very nice to Jacob. She almost acted like he was beneath her. Clara suspected it had something to do with the influence of her rich friends. They hated Jacob and thought of him as beneath them, so naturally, Katie began to see him the same way too.

"Should you take this thing off me, and I just go home?"

She could clearly see the anguish on his face. He didn't want to go. He wanted to be with her. Clara bit her lip and tried to clear her mind. She needed to put Jacob on hold for a while and deal with her daughter. Priorities first.

"For now, I think it's best you go home. Give me a few days to smooth things over with Katie and then I'll call you. We'll stick to two days like before."

"Promise?" Jacob said with hope in his eyes. "I can't bear being away from you."

"Hush up," Clara said. "I'll smooth things over with my daughter and then call you. In the meantime, your punishment continues."

"It does?" Jacob grinned weakly.

She let her gaze drift down his muscular chest and broad shoulders. Katie was making a mistake, Clara thought, despite his obvious and glaring flaws. Perhaps if she was careful, she could still salvage the situation, but it would take time and finesse. It would be such a waste of a fine young man just to toss him to the curb because he likes to jerk off.

"Get going," Clara said. "I'll call you in two days. In the meantime, you will stay caged. I'm not entirely done with you. Despite what just happened, I want to see this through."

That was all Jacob needed to hear. He opened his mouth to say something but then closed it. His eyes said it all anyway, and Clara understood. He darted out of Katie's room and down the stairs.

Returning to her bedroom, Clara tossed her bathrobe and found more acceptable clothing. She looked at herself in the mirror and briefly wondered what a guy like Jacob even saw in her. She wondered what anyone saw in her. She felt like a horrible mother and a selfish person. She didn't know the answers to the questions in her mind, but she knows she had to be careful now. Her heart was divided now with Jacob on one side and Katie on the other.

"That boy is nothing but trouble," Clara told herself in the mirror, not realizing she wore a smile. When she went downstairs, Jacob and his clothes, were already gone.

Shared by Katie's Mom

How hard could two days of wearing a cock cage be? That's what Clara commanded him to do. Not that he had much choice in the matter since Clara held the key. Jacob thought her request would be an easy thing to do, and it was, for the first day. The ruined orgasm Clara had given him was so intense that he needed a full day just to recover, so day one was a cinch.

On the second day, however, things got a little more difficult, and Jacob was beginning to suffer. Washing and cleaning himself in the shower was easy. The cock cage allowed soap and water to do its job, which was good he supposed. But that damn cage prevented him from stroking off–which was part of his daily routine until now.

While sitting in his apartment, alone, Jacob's mind began to wonder. So much had happened over the last few days, from first spying on Clara in the shower to being tied to a chair while Clara teased him. Every thought aroused him, and there was nothing he could do about it.

Each time his mind replayed images, his cock responded, and his balls became painfully squeezed between the base plate and connecting ring. Even if he managed to endure the squeezing, the cock cage itself didn't have enough space to allow him to become fully erect. The pain and lack of space eventually killed his growing erection leaving him unable to get hard.

How hard were two days in a cock cage? In truth, it was agony.

Feeling frustrated and horny, Jacob stormed around his apartment thinking of ways to get the cock cage off. The golden lock held firm despite his best efforts to pick it open. Without Clara's key, he was never going to find relief. He was at her mercy.

Part of him wanted to pick up the phone and call Clara, but her instructions were to wait until she called him. She was smoothing things over with Katie and needed time. While stewing on the couch, Jacob realized that losing Katie didn't even bother him. She was a terrible girlfriend, and he resented being the only one who even tried to make it work. She was aloof and snobby the entire time they dated, and he couldn't recall one instance where they were romantic or intimate together. *Well fuck her*, he fumed. He only stuck it out with Katie so he could be closer to her mom, Clara.

In the frustration of trying to find relief, Jacob decided to clean his apartment. It wasn't a fancy apartment, but he liked it. Both his parent's lived out of state and helped him with the rent while he was in college. He liked San Altra, and he liked living near the beach which, until he first met Clara, was a favorite place to watch beautiful women. From his rusty balcony, he could see the blue ocean and smell the salty breeze. With the proper binoculars, he could people watch the beach from the comfort of his balcony. Well, bikini watch was probably a more accurate term.

With his apartment cleaned, Jacob once more struggled not to think about Clara or his sexual adventures over the past few days. He wanted to, but each time his mind went there, his cock painfully expanded, squeezing his balls like a vice. It turned out to be the longest day of his life.

* * *

"Are you going to sit there and pout all day?" Clara finally broke down and said to Katie after neither of them spoke to each other for a full day.

"What is there to say?" Katie retorted. "You stole my boyfriend."

Clara threw her hands in the air and stormed into the kitchen, leaving Katie to fume alone in the living room. She was tempted to call Jacob, but the two days weren't over, and Jacob needed to get accustomed to his cock cage. Every time she tried to imagine the torture he was going through; Clara found herself growing aroused. Was he squirming in his bed, unable to find release? What thoughts were going through his mind? Was he angry? She hoped he wasn't.

She would give him a full two days to suffer before resuming contact and his training. In the meantime, she had yet to make a dent in Katie's pouty demeanor. What she needed was a calm, grown-up conversation with her daughter, to explain once again what happened and why. As Clara started a kettle to make some tea, she remembered Jackie's warning: Katie would think her mother had sex with her boyfriend, and it would crush her.

A short time later, Clara carried two steaming mugs of mint tea laced with honey back into the living room and set one beside her daughter. Putting her mug on a coaster, Clara sat across from her daughter.

"You can't stay angry forever," Clara said. It was a warning shot across the bow. She was going to iron this out.

Katie glanced at the mug of steaming tea, her eyes staring blankly.

"I'm sorry for what Jacob did," Clara continued after a moment. "There is no excuse for his actions, but you must understand I was trying to take care of the situation before it got out of hand."

A grunt escaped Katie's lips, and she shook her head.

"Would you rather I called the police? Would you have been happier if I came right out and told everyone what had happened? How would your friend's have felt knowing Jacob took advantage of their vulnerabilities and watched them topless? They would have snitched to their parents, their friends; your entire social circle would know. The rumors would spread. People would look at you and say; there's Katie, who's boyfriend jerked off at her pool party."

"I want to believe you had the best intentions, mom, I really do. But I can't stop thinking about your stained panties in my garbage can. If what you say is true, then why did you sleep with him?"

So that was the linchpin; those damn panties, Clara thought. She thinks Jacob, and I had sex. Clara had to admit she was caught off guard when Katie pulled her soiled panties out of the trash. Of all the things she did with Jacob, though, she never had intercourse. She thought it funny being accused of the one thing she didn't do.

"I don't know how to convince you, Katie. I had no idea my panties were even there or that he had taken them. But think about it for a moment and use logic. If Jacob and I had sex, then why would we then dispose of the evidence in *your* room and *your* trash can? Wouldn't we want to hide something like that?"

Folding her arms, Katie looked up. "I don't know."

"Trust me when I say I had no idea those panties were there. Jacob confessed to spying on me too; you heard him, so I'm just as much a victim as you. Don't you think his confession and the fact the panties were in your room, give credence to the fact we never had sex?"

"He is a disgusting pig," Katie stated.

"I want to say all men are, but that's not true. Jacob has good qualities and putting aside his proclivity to masturbation he isn't that bad a guy."

Katie blinked and nearly laughed.

"What? Did I say something funny?"

"Proclivity to masturbation? Mom, who talks like that?"

Clara blinked and smiled a little. "Well, how would you describe it then?"

"He's a disgusting pig who likes to jerk off while watching girls in secret?"

Clara shook her head. "Too many words. He has a proclivity to masturbation. It sounds much better."

"Yeah, if you're writing an erotic story," Katie smiled.

There was a pregnant pause as both women sipped their tea and glanced around the empty living room.

Clara leaned forward. "Trust me, I never had sexual relations with that man."

"Me neither," Katie confessed.

"What? You never had sex? Not once?"

Katie shook her head. "No, mom. It's the honest truth. I didn't want to get pregnant and end up like you–no offense. I love you, and you're a great mom, but I want my life to be different. I don't want to end up pregnant in my teens like you did. Trust me, though, he wanted sex, but I never gave in."

Clara sat back and looked at her daughter in a different light. "I'm proud of you, sweetie. I just assumed, because how handsome he is, that you two were sexually active."

"Nope. We kissed once, but that's about it. Did you know he's a virgin too?"

Clara wished she hadn't been sipping her tea when she heard those words. Her eyes grew wide in shock, and she very nearly spit out a mouthful of tea. Setting the cup down, Clara wiped her hands and stared at her daughter.

"Jacob is a virgin?"

Katie smirked. "And so am I, mom. Thanks for being shocked about that too."

"That explains so much," Clara said as she frowned in thought.

"What do you mean?"

"He's a twenty-year-old virgin in the prime of his sexual life, and he's never had sex. No wonder he whacks off like a retarded monkey all the time."

Katie laughed. "Mom! Please! I didn't need the visual."

"I'm sorry," Clara said, looking at her daughter. "I'm proud of you for not having sex. I just assumed you were on the pill and using protection."

"Well, I am on the pill, but that's more a precaution, plus I get them for free with my student prescription card." Katie stopped talking and stared at her mother for a few moments. "So honest to God truth, you never slept with Jacob?"

Clara shook her head, *no.*

"I believe you," Katie said.

"What changed? Five minutes ago you were certain I had."

"No one can fake surprise like that."

"Like what?"

"When I said we were both virgins still; you were shocked. If you had been sleeping with Jacob, you would have already known he was a virgin. I could tell by your expression that you had no idea."

"So telling me," Clara observed, "was a sort of test?"

Katie nodded.

"Well, I'm glad I passed. Now can you now believe me when I say I was trying to handle his demented monkey's proclivity for masturbation?"

Laughing, Katie nodded. "Yes, I believe you, but stop talking like that!"

"It's a deal," Clara said. She grinned and then took another sip of her tea.

They were both silent for a few minutes, each with their thoughts. Finally, Katie tipped the last of her tea back and set the mug down.

"So now what?"

"What would you like to talk about?" Clara asked.

"That thing–that cock cage–did you take it off?"

"No, I left it on him," Clara answered carefully. When Katie raised an eyebrow, Clara explained further. "You broke up with him, and if I took the thing off, then he would simply have gone home and vanished forever."

"I thought that was the idea," Katie said dryly. "To get rid of him."

"And get away scot-free? Not on my watch," Clara said. "That boy deserves punishment for what he did, and if I simply let him go, then we all remain victims in a sense. Your relationship might be over, but his sentence is not."

"I wish I could punish him," Katie mused.

That was a perplexing statement and Clara leaned forward. "What do you mean?"

Shrugging, Katie thought for a moment. "It just doesn't seem fair that you get to punish him for looking at us topless and, you know, doing stuff to himself. We were all victims. I think he should be forced to confess his crime to all of us, not just you and me."

"You mean your friends?"

Katie nodded.

"They might report it to the police you know, or at the very least inform their parents. The last thing I want to do is explain to irate parents why I didn't call the police right away. Yikes, just the idea of dealing with that mess makes me cringe."

"You're probably right."

Katie chewed her lip for a moment, and Clara thought she looked somewhat worried all of a sudden. "I know that expression, Katie, what happened? Did you already tell your friends? It's bad enough they saw him practically naked. Please tell me you didn't tell everyone."

"Not everyone," Katie relented. After a moment she said, "Just one."

"Who?"

"Tiffany. I was so mad that I had to talk to someone. She's my closest friend."

Clara nodded, seeing the complications. "And she hates Jacob."

"Well, that too."

Running a hand through her brunette hair, Clara leaned back and exhaled loudly. Everyone knew how much Tiffany disliked Jacob. There was no secret there. It would take very little motivation for that girl to pick up the phone and call the cops. Clara was sure nothing would please Tiffany more than seeing Jacob hauled off to jail for indecent exposure and lewd behavior.

"I wish you hadn't told anyone," Clara said. "Especially her."

"I'm sorry, mom. I had to vent."

Waving her hand Clara nodded in understanding. "What's done is done. Can you tell me what her reaction was?"

"Pretty shocked."

"I bet. Do you think Tiffany will call the police?"

"She mentioned it, but she likes you and doesn't want you involved."

Clara rubbed her chin for a moment as an idea formed. "Can Tiffany be trusted?"

Now it was Katie's turn to be cautious. "Probably, yes. Why are you asking?"

"I just had an idea. If you call Tiffany, how soon until she can come over?"

"Well, I can ask her," Katie replied. She took her cell phone out and held it up for her mother to see. "Want me to call?"

Clara smiled and nodded.

"What should I tell her?"

"Tell her that I've had an idea for punishing Jacob, that she might like."

"She'll want details, mom."

"Just tell her it involves Jacob, and the chance to extract punishment from him. She just can't tell anyone. I think that will be enough to entice her interest. Tell her to come over right away, and we will sit down and talk about it. Tell her nothing is set in stone, I just want to get her opinion."

Katie seemed doubtful, but she nodded and dialed her friend. As Katie waited for Tiffany to pick up, she cast one last uncertain expression at Clara before moving to the kitchen and out of earshot. Clara didn't mind. Teenagers always need privacy. A few minutes later Katie returned and pocketed her phone with a smile on her face. Wouldn't you know it, Tiffany was game.

* * *

Horny wasn't the word Jacob would use to describe how he felt. He was beyond that. When Clara had first told him he would be wearing a cock cage for two days, he assumed that sometime on the second day he would be granted relief. No, Clara meant two full days and then she would call him on the third day. When the phone rang in his apartment, Jacob nearly tore the receiver off the wall in his rush to answer.

"Clara?"

"Hello, Jacob."

"Get this thing off me! Please, I'm dying here." Jacob could hear a faint chuckle from Clara. She was enjoying this!

"Is my poor little pet having a hard time learning self-control?"

Jacob clamped his mouth shut. He wouldn't give her the satisfaction of knowing just how sexually frustrated he was. Even hearing Clara's soft, sultry voice was making his cock begin to twitch. He forced his mind to think about baseball and squeezed his eyes shut. His yearning was intolerable!

"I'm sorry, but I didn't quite hear you," Clara continued, her voice sounding even more amused. "Perhaps we have a bad phone connection, and I should call back tomorrow?"

"I need this thing taken off, today. I've learned my lesson. Can I come over?"

"That's why I called, Darling. I know you're dying to find some relief but quite frankly I'm busy all morning, and I just can't help you. You'll have to wait until this afternoon. What I need to get done is far more important than your desires, so you'll just have to suffer a bit longer. Can you do that? Come over around four o'clock."

Jacob looked at his watch. It was half past eight in the morning. He'd have to endure this torture for nearly eight more hours. He ground his teeth and forced himself to remain calm.

"I can wait that long, no problem. I'll be there at four."

"Good, I have some plans for you. Don't be late or we'll have to start all over with another two full days of denial therapy. I sure hope you learn the importance of not making a woman wait. See you soon."

Jacob was about to promise he wouldn't be late, but Clara had hung up. He put the receiver back and groaned. *Eight god damn hours.* He could wait if he had too, but one thing he was certain of, he wasn't enduring this cock cage one more day.

* * *

"Tiffany! It's so nice to see you again," Clara said in greeting when she answered the door. "Please come in. Would you care for some cold lemonade? I just made a fresh container. Katie is in the pool so we can have some privacy to talk a little."

"Thank you, that would be wonderful," Tiffany replied. She was wearing a pink miniskirt, white sandals, and a white cut-off t-shirt that exposed a little of her flat midriff. A dainty white designer purse hung from her shoulder. Her long slicked back raven hair was tied in a tight ponytail. Today she only wore a light sprinkling of makeup, but Clara noticed her lipstick and nails matched her pink skirt.

Clara returned to the kitchen with Tiffany in tow and grabbed a tall glass from the cupboard. She fetched two ice cubes from the freezer and dropped them into the cup. The lemonade pitcher was on the counter, and Tiffany watched as Clara carefully poured her glass.

"I'm curious," Tiffany said, her sharp features turning thoughtful as she sat on a stool. "Is Jacob here right now?"

"No, I sent him home three days ago. Here you go." Clara set the glass on a coaster in front of Tiffany.

"Thank you. May I ask another question?"

Clara nodded and poured herself a glass as well.

"When I last saw Jacob, he was wearing what Katie told me later is a cock cage. Is he still wearing it? I'm only asking because I did some research online. Being purely curious and all. I've never heard of such a thing before."

After downing half her lemonade, Clara set the glass down and took a seat on a kitchen stool opposite Tiffany and gave her full attention.

"Yes, he is still wearing the cage," Clara began. "I'm not sure what Katie explained to you over the phone, but you are aware that I caught Jacob masturbating in my upstairs office?"

"Yes, she told me," Tiffany said, her tone conveying her obvious disgust. She wrinkled her nose in disdain. "You caught him peeping when we were topless in the pool. I can't say I'm shocked. Jacob might be a handsome guy, but he lacks proper upbringing."

Clara raised an eyebrow.

Leaning closer, Tiffany confided in a low whisper, "Just between you and me I don't think Jacob was suitable for Katie. I told her that from the start."

"Is that so?" Clara said.

Sitting upright, Tiffany nodded promptly. She picked up her drink and took a dainty sip before carefully setting it back down. "Most definitely. Even without his moral faults, he just wasn't good enough for our Katie. He has no future."

Clara took another drink and said nothing.

"So, Katie tells me you have a plan or something to punish Jacob?"

"I do. At first, I was going to keep this just between Jacob and me, but once my daughter discovered what happened and then told you, I've decided we should all play a part in making Jacob a better man. No one else knows what happened."

Tiffany snorted. "I'm not sure making Jacob better is even possible. But what did you have in mind?"

Clara began to explain her idea. As she spoke, Tiffany moved from mildly skeptical to intrigued, until, in the end, she was enthusiastic.

"You're sure Katie won't have a problem with this?" Tiffany asked.

"It was actually her idea," Clara confessed.

A giggle escaped Tiffany as she shook her head in disbelief. "I should have known there was more to Katie than simply a good girl persona."

"So are you in?"

"Oh, I'm in alright," Tiffany said with a wicked grin. "No one outside our little circle will ever find out, though, right?"

"I promise," Clara said masking her amusement.

"Where is Jacob now?"

"At home," Clara answered. "He won't be here until four o'clock."

"Great. Say hello to Katie for me. I need to run home and get a few things. I'll be back around three or so. I don't want to miss this."

"I'll tell her you said hello. Remember, though, not a word about this to any of your friends," Clara warned. "Our purpose is to teach Jacob a lesson."

Tiffany stood and drained her glass. When she set it down, her sharp features were focused. "Oh, I plan on teaching Jacob a lesson he'll never forget. Thank you for the lemonade, it was delish."

"My pleasure," Clara said casually and watched Tiffany walk towards the front door. There was a moment of hesitation in her mind though. She weighed the wisdom of including Tiffany in her designs, but it was too late to change her plans now. Besides, Clara reasoned, if she had kept Tiffany in the dark and not included her, then who knows what rumors that girl might spread. Bringing Tiffany in would probably guarantee her silence. As Clara watched Tiffany close the door, she felt a tiny stab of pity for Jacob. That poor boy had no idea what was in store for him.

* * *

Four o'clock couldn't come fast enough for Jacob, and when he arrived at Clara's house, with time to spare, he sat eagerly in his car and waited. With a minute until the allotted time he got out of his car and waited next to the front door staring at his watch. He didn't want to be late and incur another two days of his cock being locked away. At four o'clock on the dot, he rang the doorbell and tried to contain his eagerness. Relief was just around the corner, and he wondered what sexy games Clara had in store for him. First, he had to get the damn cage off.

When Katie answered the door, Jacob's smile slid from his face, and he stepped back in alarm. He wasn't expecting to see his ex-girlfriend. Had Clara smoothed things over with Katie? He didn't know. Her gaze seemed frosty as she looked him up and down.

"Come to fuck my mom now?" Katie asked in a haughty tone.

"Katie, I wasn't expecting you. I'm not here to do that, but even if I was, what business is it of yours? You dumped me, remember? I don't need to explain myself to you but for your information, I'm here to get this thing taken off," Jacob explained gesturing towards his shorts.

Stepping back, Katie opened the door wider. She didn't say a word but merely nodded towards the kitchen. Jacob stepped through the doorway cautiously keeping an eye on his ex-girlfriend. He didn't think she would stab him or anything, but she was unpredictable in his mind.

"Oh look, the manservant is here," Tiffany exclaimed from the kitchen stool she was sitting on. "And very punctual too." There was mirth in her eyes mixed with cruelty.

"Hello," Jacob said with a roll of his eyes, wondering why Snorter was here. He spotted Clara the moment she walked down the stairs. He stopped and caught the scent of her perfume as she passed him on her way to the kitchen. She was wearing a white skirt with little blue dots and a navy blue blouse. Her long hair was pulled back, like it often was, and tied in a ponytail. He felt his heart quicken with longing as he gazed at her.

"Good afternoon, Jacob," Clara said as she turned and leaned against the kitchen counter. "Come closer, we won't bite. I was just setting up the chair you'll be using."

Jacob hesitated and glanced at Tiffany and Katie.

"Don't worry about them," Clara explained. "Would you care for a drink? I made some fruit punch."

"Um, no thank you," Jacob replied. He ventured into the kitchen and watched as Katie took a seat next to Tiffany before seating himself at a safe distance. *What was going on here?* He still wasn't sure if Clara and Katie had smoothed things over, and the presence of Tiffany put him on edge.

"How does it feel wearing a cock cage for three days?" Tiffany asked with a cruel smile. She leaned forward and rested her elbows on the counter.

Jacob blinked and peered at Clara who was watching him keenly.

"Well?" Katie said. "Answer us."

"It's been difficult," Jacob said slowly, deciding to keep his cards close to the vest and see what was going on before venturing too much.

"I asked Tiffany to be here," Clara said. Jacob looked perplexed, so she continued, "I think you have something you need to confess to her."

Raising an eyebrow, Jacob finally understood. Part of his punishment was to confess his crime to the one friend Katie had who really despised him. He swallowed hard and slowly nodded.

Tiffany was all smiles as she waited.

"The day after Katie's birthday," Jacob said. "I watched you topless in the pool with everyone else."

"Go on," Clara ordered after it became clear that Jacob wasn't offering more details.

"I got excited and jerked off. Katie's mom caught me, and that's why I'm wearing this cage thing. Its punishment."

Tiffany shook her head in disgust. "I always knew you were bad news."

Jacob bit his tongue and said nothing.

"Because Tiffany is as much a victim in this as the rest of us," Clara stated as she stepped closer and folded her arms under her firm breasts. "I have taken the liberty of including her in your punishment."

Jacob's heart sank. He glanced at Tiffany and then at Katie. Both girls were smirking in triumph, obviously intent on carrying out some torture. Was he to be tied down and given to Tiffany? The idea made him cringe.

"I see," Jacob finally said.

"Come with me," Clara said as she headed for the stairs.

Jacob cast one last glance at Katie and Tiffany then averted his eyes. He trudged behind Clara, not even bothering to steal a peek at her shapely legs as he followed her up the stairs. His heart was racing, but more out of fear than of excitement. How was Tiffany going to punish him?

Clara led him to Katie's bedroom which surprised Jacob. He was expecting Clara to take him to her bedroom. In Katie's doorway, he spotted the familiar kitchen chair facing the bed and a variety of Clara's sex toys, ropes and whips laid neatly on the mattress.

"Take off your clothes and sit," Clara ordered.

"Can we talk first? I missed you."

His words had an effect on her. Clara seemed startled and turned to look into his eyes. "You missed me?"

Jacob nodded. "I couldn't stop thinking of you, not even for a moment."

Her hard features softened, and she reached out and touched his arm.

Jacob felt his face flush as he stepped closer and took Clara in his arms. She blinked in surprise but didn't fight his advance. With their face inches apart, Jacob drank in her beauty and then kissed her.

She seemed startled at his boldness at first, then wrapped her arms around his broad shoulders and returned his kiss with one of her own. He smiled, and she wanted to smother him with more kisses, but she regained her composure and forced him back.

"I missed you too."

"Before we start roleplaying, Clara, can I just ask why Tiffany and Katie are here? Were you able to patch things over?"

Clara thought for a moment and gave him a short nod. "It wasn't easy. Katie is really angry, and she thinks we had sex."

"I wish we had."

"Hush," Clara put a finger to her lips. "We have to be careful. She hasn't figured out what to make of you and me. I had to bring Tiffany in—"

"Why?"

"—because Katie spilled the beans to her. I had no choice. Otherwise, we risk Tiffany telling her parents or Katie's other friends."

With their first kiss out of the way, Jacob felt bolder. He gently caressed the side of Clara's face before nodding. "I don't want Tiffany taking..."

"Your virginity?" Clara said softly. When Jacob's eyes grew wide, she smiled and placed her hand over his. "I know. Katie told me. I'm proud of you for respecting her wishes to stay a virgin. I guess you had a lot of pent-up frustrations keeping your hands off my daughter."

"I struggled from time to time," Jacob confessed.

"Why the long face?"

"I feel stupid. I didn't want you to know I'm a twenty-year-old virgin. But I don't want to lose it to Tiffany. I can't let her be my first and spend my whole life knowing *she* took it. Can you promise she won't have sex with me?"

Clara pulled him closer and felt his strong arms wrap around her. "Jacob, I don't know what to say. I promise."

"About what?" he whispered into her ear.

"You are such a strange man. You seem too tender and caring at times. You respected my daughter by not having sex, and yet you have a proclivity to masturbation which seems so juvenile. I don't know what to make of you."

"I'm just a guy who's fallen in love with a beautiful woman," Jacob said. He held her at arms length and smiled. "I can't help it. Promise me that Tiffany won't pop my cherry. I'm saving it for you."

Clara thought his heartfelt confession was adorable, but she had to laugh at his choice of words in expressing it. She placed a hand on his muscular chest. "I promise when the time comes, I will gladly be your first. Now get undressed and let's get you tied up."

* * *

When Clara returned to the kitchen, Both Katie and Tiffany looked at her expectantly. Without saying a word, Clara poured a glass of fruit punch and drank it down. Once the glass was empty, she turned towards Tiffany setting the glass on the counter.

"He is bound and waiting."

Tiffany clapped her hands and looked at Katie briefly.

"So I can do anything I want with him?"

Katie rolled her eyes.

"There is one limit, though," Clara cautioned. "No penetration."

Tiffany made a funny face. "Oh, yuck, never. Don't worry about that. I plan on teasing him. Can I unlock his cage?"

"You are going to give him a ruined orgasm?" Katie asked.

Clara handed the small golden key over. "Don't lose this."

"I might give him that, or I might just tease him. I'm definitely not going to fuck him. Yuck. I don't have sex with my friend's ex-boyfriends. Please. I have standards you know."

"We weren't suggesting otherwise," Clara said.

"Just make sure he suffers," Katie said. Her comment gave Clara pause.

"Take as much time as you need," Clara added. "Perhaps Katie and I will lounge beside the pool. Come out and get us when you're done."

Tiffany grinned and clutched the key. "Wish me luck."

As Tiffany all but bounded for the stairs, Katie glanced at her mother with a concerned look. Clara shrugged and poured another glass. Whatever happened upstairs, she didn't want to know about it. She just hoped Tiffany didn't change her mind and steal Jacob's virginity. She kept her thoughts to herself, though, as she led Katie through the living room and out the patio door. Jacob's virginity was her's to take—she wasn't sharing that with anyone, Clara mused. She planned on enjoying every moment of it when the time came.

* * *

Knowing what was about to happen and being helpless put Jacob on edge. His heart thumped as if he'd just run a race and his mind kept repeating one word: Tiffany. After Clara had bound him to the chair leaving nothing but his cock cage on, Jacob had time to think. Being bound and helpless was still a strange sensation, and the feeling was amplified all the more knowing Tiffany was going to have her way with him. All he could do was wait. Of all Katie's friends, why did it have to be Tiffany? What sort of punishment would she inflict? Despite detesting the girl, he couldn't deny that Tiffany was damn sexy–even if she had fake tits. He knew she held no love for him and recalled all the times she mocked or teased or peered at him with those haughty eyes. Now at her mercy, he feared her true colors would show.

With his back to the door, he hadn't heard Tiffany enter the bedroom until he heard the unmistakable click of the door. He had no idea if she had just arrived, or had been standing observing him for a while before shutting the door. Turning in the chair, Jacob tried to gauge her mood. Would she be playful? He doubted that, but he could hope. When he saw that Tiffany was alone, and Katie wasn't with her, his alarm became more urgent. Yikes, he thought, this could be bad.

"Hello, manservant," Tiffany said in a condescending tone.

"Mistress," Jacob replied as calmly as he could.

Her eyes rose in mild surprise, and she decided she liked her title. Sauntering to the bed, Tiffany gathered the neatly laid out items and set them aside. She reclined on the bed, her head propped by her arm. With cool eyes, Tiffany gazed at her bound victim.

Jacob remained stoic and silent.

"I like it when you call me Mistress," Tiffany said at last. She appeared calm and not in any hurry. Being alone with a bound and helpless man didn't seem to phase her at all.

"I am to be punished, Mistress?"

Tiffany's sly smile grew toothy. "Oh yes. But seeing that you are respectful and have learned your place, I will delay your suffering for a while."

"Whatever Mistress desires," Jacob said. He would take whatever reprieve she gave him to build up his courage. He didn't want to flinch or appear weak to her in any way because that would only serve to confirm her opinion of him. He would show her that he could take whatever she dished out and more. There was no way he would show fear.

"Tell me, *Manservant*," Tiffany said, stressing his new title, "I've been curious ever since Katie told me what her mom found you doing. Why did you jerk off while watching us?"

So it was an interrogation, Jacob thought. He could handle questions. He made a note not to reveal his feelings for Clara. Anything he said to Tiffany would no doubt find a way to Katie's ear, and he didn't want to inflame any hurt feelings between mother and daughter. Tiffany appeared to be relaxing on the bed, but Jacob noticed her eyes were sharp, and had no doubts that her devious mind was recording every word.

"At first, I was just curious," Jacob began. "When I saw Katie and all of you around the pool in your bikinis, I became aroused. I'll admit that. I thought if I walked outside to join you with a gigantic erection in my pants, then I'd be ridiculed." It wasn't the truth, but it was all his mind could conjure to explain his actions. Upon reflection, he had never considered the consequences of walking outside at the pool party with an erection.

"Go on," Tiffany said.

"Well, there isn't much more to say. I went upstairs to find a good vantage point and kind of spanked the monkey a little."

"How vulgar. You missed telling me the most important part though."

"Which is?"

"Did you look at my tits while you jerked off?"

Jacob blinked in surprise. He wasn't expecting that kind of question. His answer died in his throat when he saw Tiffany slide a hand under the waistband of her short skirt. When she looked up and saw his eyes watching, her hand abruptly stopped and withdrew.

"Are you turned on?" Tiffany asked, her cheeks flushing slightly.

Jacob tried to portray disinterest but with his cock betrayed him. Two days of denial had made him easily aroused despite what his mind thought. As his erection grew, the pressure on his testicles counteracted his arousal. With effort and concentration, his erection subsided, and the pain stopped.

"I'm not happy that didn't my questions, Jacob. Is there something wrong?" Tiffany unhooked her skirt and slid it down her long legs. She was wearing sheer white panties with lace accents that left nothing to the imagination. From what

Jacob could tell, before averting his eyes, she shaved everything down there.

"I'm sorry, Mistress, but I was distracted," Jacob said, and it was the truth. Despite a general dislike of her, he found Tiffany's body to be quite alluring. He didn't even know you could buy panties that revealing. They were no doubt very expensive.

Tiffany tilted her head and regarded him with interest. "You seem to be in some discomfort, manservant. Is that thing hard to wear?"

Jacob nodded.

"Would you like me to unlock your poor little cock?" She suddenly dangled the golden key in her fingers, "I have permission to use this."

"If it pleases, Mistress," Jacob said. He made a mental note not to beg.

With a girlish giggle, Tiffany slid off the bed. Jacob was expecting her to unlock him right away, but instead, she inspected his bindings. When he glanced at her, Tiffany snorted.

"I just want to be sure you can't escape and grab me. Men like you cannot be trusted, so girls like me have to take precautions."

Rolling his eyes, Jacob nodded. He doubted caution ever entered her mind. She was a spoiled rich prissy girl who got whatever she wanted.

At last satisfied he was secured, Tiffany reached for the golden padlock on his cock cage, inserted the key and with a twist, clicked it open. She pulled the tubular section away and then wiggled the base plate off. At last, his cock was free, and it responded with vigor, quickly growing and stretching stiff. Jacob couldn't help but groan in relief. It felt good finally achieving a full erection. Opening his eyes he was about to thank her, but then remembered who it was and decided against it. He would never thank her for anything.

"That's much better. Fair is fair. You got to see my tits, and now I get to see your cock," Tiffany said as she leaned against Katie's bed.

Jacob let his eyes travel up her long slender legs to her frilly white panties. To his surprise, Tiffany suddenly peeled off her top and unlatched her bra. She blushed a little as she slipped her panties down and stood naked in front of him. For someone so offended that he had looked at her bare breasts, Jacob was surprised at how quickly she had stripped. Tiffany put her hands on her hips and regarded his cock with interest.

"I would like to feel a cock that big inside of me, but Clara said no penetration. I will respect her wishes," Tiffany said. "You see, unlike you, I'm able to show self-control. Besides, I'd most likely end up pregnant like Clara did the first time she had sex and the thought of having your baby in me is revolting."

Jacob reeled in shock, but his face remained passive.

"So answer my questions," Tiffany said. "And I might reward you with pleasure, but don't get your hopes up for sex. I still think you're a disgusting pig and I would never let someone like you fuck me."

Gee thanks for the compliment.

"What would you like to know?" Jacob asked. He stared openly at her bare breasts and delicate bare pussy lips, unable to decide which he liked more. His cock was hard already, so there was no point in trying to ignore her allure.

"When you jerked off watching us in the pool. Did you look at my tits?"

"Of course, I did, they are spectacular," Jacob lied. In truth, he hated fake tits, but she was in control, and perhaps flattery might soften whatever punishment she had in mind. His words worked it appeared as Tiffany grinned and gave her silicone breasts a little squeeze.

"They are nice, aren't they?"

Jacob nodded with suitable enthusiasm.

"Better than Katie's boobs?"

Did it matter? He guessed her vanity was a weakness and played along. "Your boobs are amazing. I haven't seen their equal."

"Oh, now you're mocking me. My tits aren't that great. Are they?"

"I would do anything to touch them," Jacob continued.

Tiffany held up a finger. "You're trying to trick me into untying you. It won't work. I'm smarter than you, Jacob."

He strongly doubted that statement, but he pretended to be ashamed of her astuteness.

"Do you know why Clara and Katie let me come up here and be alone with you?"

"To punish me?"

"Yes, but I think that's just a cover. What I think is Katie wants me to fuck you because she never did. I bet she is dying to know what she missed. I also think Clara wants to ruin my life by getting me pregnant. That's why she used reverse psychology and forbade me from fucking you. She wants us to have sex. I know she does. I don't think Clara likes me."

That's because Clara is a good judge of character. "Your powers of deduction are incredible," Jacob said. "I'm impressed. If we had sex I would probably get your pregnant, you're right about that. She must have been trying to trick you."

"Thank you, manservant," Tiffany said with a smile. "Don't think all your sweet talking is going to get you out of punishment, though. I just never punished a boy before, so you'll have to forgive me for not being sure what to do."

"I understand," Jacob said calmly. "I'm new at this too."

As if deciding something, Tiffany crawled onto the bed and reclined on her shoulders. She peered at him, then asked, "Would you like to see my pussy?"

"Yes, I would," Jacob said and was surprised he wasn't lying.

Her face blushed a little as she regarded him for a moment longer. She seemed hesitant to spread her legs like she was toying with the idea and it excited her. After a moment she spread her legs slowly, her eyes watching him for a reaction.

Over two full days in a cock cage had created a lot of sexual frustration for Jacob, and the sight of Tiffany's spread pink pussy sent him into hyperarousal. His cock throbbed, and he found himself trying to lean forward. Tiffany saw his reaction and quickly closed her legs with a giggle.

"You like it?"

Jacob closed his eyes and moaned.

"I'll take that as a yes. Do you want your stiff hard cock inside me? I will if you want me to."

Feeling the last of his resolve fading, Jacob nodded in shame. He wanted to hold out for Clara but his urge to find release was too strong.

Tiffany swung her legs over the side of the bed and sat up. "I knew you would. Well tough, my pussy isn't for your type. Do you think I'd let some poor guy like you fuck rich girl pussy? In your dreams. You are beneath me, and despite how impressive your cock is, I can't let someone with your social status think they can have a pussy like this."

Jacob raised an eyebrow and wondered if Tiffany believed what she was saying. She was raised rich, had won't for nothing in her life, had never lifted a finger to work and as a result thought she was better than everyone. She was the embodiment of everything he thought was wrong in society.

"Ahh, I see being denied caused your cock to wilt a little," Tiffany said.

Jacob closed his eyes and looked away. He could feel his sexual yearning drain from his body. After hearing her most elite comments, all attraction vanished.

"Open your eyes and look at me," Tiffany ordered.

Taking a deep breath, Jacob opened his eyes. He focused for a second on Katie's horrible collection of stuffed animals before turning to face the spoiled rich girl sitting naked in front of him.

"Good manservant. I want to masturbate while watching you, just like you did while watching me. Should I use a vibrator or a rubber cock?"

Jacob bit his tongue. He wasn't in a good position to speak his mind. Realizing he was still trapped and tied to a chair, he would have to endure whatever she decided.

"Well?"

"Why not use both, Mistress," Jacob offered just to shut her up.

"What a novel idea. Thank you, manservant," Tiffany cooed. She selected a flesh colored silicone cock and a small vibrator and held them up for him to inspect.

Jacob remained silent. Was he supposed to give her his blessing or be impressed with how 'big' her small toys were?

"If you're a good boy and behave yourself, perhaps I'll give you a hand job or something. Would you like that?"

Hoping his disdain passed for frustration, Jacob nodded.

Flipping on the little vibrator, Tiffany giggled as it buzzed in her hand. She closed her eyes and spread her knees parting her moist pussy. Placing the little vibrator against her clit, Tiffany gasped, and her eyes flew open and focused on Jacob's face. She pressed the tip of the silicone cock against her opening and moved it back and forth in little circles.

Despite being disgusted with who she was as a person, Jacob couldn't help but feel intrigued watching Tiffany maneuver and play with her sex toys. *This is how rich girls*

masturbate? With little designer toys and expensive vibrators?
Jacob let his curiosity get the better of him, and his body
responded. His wilting erection slowed to a stop, paused with
indecision for a while and then began to grow again. She
might be a terrible person, he reasoned, but he couldn't help
his arousal at watching a hot college girl play with herself.

Tiffany worked the silicone cock up and down the length of
her small pussy while twirling the vibrator over her clit. Her
mouth made a small "O" briefly. She bit her lip and slipped
the cock between her wet folds which parted and gripped the
toy like a glove.

"Do you like watching me masturbate?" Tiffany whispered,
her voice tinged with arousal.

Jacob didn't lie when he nodded.

She liked his response and moved both the vibrator and the
cock faster, her breath catching. Though she was on her
backside, her fake breasts barely moved, and Jacob could see
her small pink nipples standing erect and firm. Fake or not, at
that moment he wanted to suck them badly. His neglected
cock ached to find release.

Tiffany's hand pumped faster, and she held the vibrator
firmly against her clit as her first orgasm came. It didn't take
long, and Jacob found it arousing to watch. She quivered and
her legs began to shake as her body made small convulsions
and her eyes rolled back. She gasped and panted and then
buried the cock as deep as it would go while resuming the
small twirls with the vibrator.

She might be a spoiled rich girl, Jacob thought, but she sure
knows how to cum hard. He waited, wondering if she would

stop or keep going. Tiffany flipped the vibrator off and brought her legs together, the cock still buried to the hilt inside of her soaked pussy. She closed her eyes and put her arm over her flushed face and let her breathing return to normal.

Jacob could only gaze at her body and wait. He could use a hand job right about now, he thought. He debated begging, but he refused to give in now. Resorting to begging is what Tiffany wanted him to do, and he wouldn't give her the satisfaction. Instead, he thought of Clara and imagined her body glistening with water in the shower. He smiled, and Tiffany thought it was because of her.

"I could fuck you right now, I'm that horny," Tiffany said, her eyes filled with uncontrolled desire as she sat upright and gazed at his hard cock.

Forcing the words out, Jacob pretended to beg. "Please, I need to fuck you, Tiffany. I can't hold out any longer. I need to cum in you."

Tiffany's countenance changed as she glared. "Ha! That's what you want, isn't it? I knew it. You want to get me pregnant. Well, forget it. I'm not opening my legs for a lowly boy like you."

Jacob lowered his eyes in what he hoped was a suitable shame.

"In fact, I'm done here now. You've seen quite enough of me already. I hope you got a good look and remembered it well because someday you'll find some welfare queen with saggy tits and a tattoo of her ex-husband on her back and wish she had my body."

Peering up, Jacob pouted. "What about a blowjob?"

"Eww gross!" Tiffany cried. She gathered her clothes and started to dress.

"I'm suffering here, Tiffany. I'll settle for a hand job. Please!"

The more he begged, the more disgusted Tiffany was with him and the more pleased he was with himself. He wondered if she felt disgusted for masturbating in front of a guy she so clearly below her station in life. If she did, Jacob was certain she would never mention it to anyone. As he watched her dress, Jacob kept firing barbs.

"I've been locked up for so long, Tiffany. Can I at least cum on your tits?"

When she finished dressing, Tiffany picked up the two sex toys she used so she could clean them in the bathroom. Turning, she regarded Jacob with scorn.

"You're a disgusting pervert, and I'm glad Katie dumped you."

Jacob wasn't expecting her vehemence, and he blinked in surprise. "I made you cum, though," he taunted. "And if I wasn't tied up in this chair, I could have done a lot more you pompous little bitch."

She jabbed a finger in his chest. "If I ever find out you told anyone what just happened here, trust me, I will hunt you down like the dog you are and ruin your miserable life."

"Ruin my life? I'm not looking to date you, but thanks. So that's a definite no to a blowjob then? Don't you want to taste the cum of a common man?"

Tiffany shrieked in disgust and stormed out of the bedroom, leaving Jacob alone and still strapped to the chair. He could hear her slam the bathroom door, and he smiled and after a moment he laughed. Mission accomplished.

As punishments go, he had survived that one pretty well he thought.

* * *

It was nearly twenty minutes later when Clara looked in on Jacob and cried in shock. He was still tied to the chair. She gasped and rushed to his side.

"I'm so sorry, sweetie, I thought Tiffany had untied you before she left."

Jacob's hands and feet were reddish from the lack of circulation, and he ached, but she smiled as Clara undid his restraints. She had called him sweetie.

"Nope, she just left me here."

"Tiffany left with Katie ten minutes ago. They seemed in a rush. I just assumed they untied you, and you were in the shower or something. This is all my fault, darling, I should have come upstairs right away."

"Tiffany, it turns out, hasn't warmed up to my charms yet. Thank you, though. So you thought I was in the shower?"

Clara nodded as she worked on the knots in the rope.

"And you decided to check up on me?"

Clara paused and looked up. She tried to keep a straight face but broke into a naughty smile. "Maybe. Would that have been so bad?"

Clara released his ankle restraint and sat back. She placed a hand on his bare leg and shook her head, her eyes filled with concern. "I'm sorry, Jacob. I had no idea she just abandoned you."

"I'll be okay. I think Tiffany enjoyed herself."

Clara's eyes flickered downward. "Did you, um, have a good orgasm?"

He couldn't help but detect a little envy or perhaps jealousy in Clara's tone. It told him that she wasn't all that wild about leaving him in Tiffany's clutches. Jealousy meant feelings. Was the woman of his dreams finally warming up to him? Jacob could only wish.

"I didn't cum."

His words startled Clara, and she turned away to mask her surprise. She stood and fussed over the pink comforter, rearranging the sex toys on the bed before glancing over her shoulder. "Why not?"

"Apparently, Tiffany thinks I'm beneath her status. She rubbed one out on the bed but ignored me."

"I'm sorry. I thought letting Tiffany in on all this was a bad idea in the first place. So, she didn't, you know, have any sex with you?"

"I'm still a virgin if that's what you're getting at," Jacob teased.

"What? That? No. That's none of my business. I was just... I mean, I wanted to make sure after so long being denied, that, you know, that your needs were taken care of. Were they?"

Jacob grinned openly. "No, I said, I didn't have an orgasm."

"Would you be willing to—"

"To have sex with you? Yes," Jacob said finishing her sentence with strength in his voice and determination on his face.

Clara blushed. "Sorry, that wasn't what I was about to say, but thank you."

"It wasn't? Oh shit." Jacob's eyes grew wide. "Shit, I'm sorry."

Clara laughed and put her hand on his shoulder. It was warm. "Look at me chattering like a little school girl too nervous to ask a boy to prom. It's just that I'm—"

"Nervous?" Jacob offered. He hoped she didn't remove her hand.

"Well that too, but what I meant was," she paused to center her thoughts before continuing. "Okay. What I mean is being near you like this affects me. I seem to find words a little difficult. I just want you to know I'm not normally like this."

"If I didn't know better, I'd say you are getting the hots for me," Jacob said as he stood and stretched his naked body in front of Clara and giving her a full show of his tanned muscles. He'd been in that chair too long.

"Well, I seem to see you naked a lot lately," Clara said.

"I like being naked around you. So does my cock."

Clara regarded him with a puzzled look.

"What?" Jacob asked.

"You can be so sweet and charming one moment and then ruin it the next by speaking. Jacob, I don't know what to make of you sometimes," Clara said.

"Can I have a hug?"

"What? Have you lost your mind? Put some clothes on."

Crestfallen, Jacob looked around the room. "Where are my clothes?"

"I put them in my bedroom."

"No wonder I'm naked all the time, you keep hiding my stuff," Jacob said as he headed towards Clara's bedroom. When Clara reached out and touched his arm, he stopped and turned.

"I've decided on one more punishment for you. Well, more of a punishment and reward mixed. Okay, not a punishment at all," Clara explained.

Despite being just scolded, Jacob had to laugh. "Whatever are you talking about?"

"I've decided to share you with another woman. Again. Right now."

Cautiously nodding, Jacob folded his arms and waited. "Who is it this time?"

Clara blushed and decided to push onward. "Jackie."

Jacob blinked. "Your Jackie? The blonde woman with big..."

"Yes," Clara said firmly. "And they're not that big."

"Why her? I only met her once, at Katie's party. You know I'm a virgin still right? And I was hoping to save it for someone special. That I care for."

"Calm down," Clara said in a soothing voice. She stepped closer and peered into his eyes. "I know your feelings for me. To be honest, I'm falling for you pretty hard too."

"So why share me with Jackie? Sure she's hot, but Clara, I want you. How much longer do I have to play this game?"

Clara tilted her head and traced a finger across his muscular chest. "Jackie is my best friend, and she knows a lot more about sex than I do. She promised me she wouldn't take your virginity, not that it's my decision who you give it to."

"Then why be with her at all? Why can't it just be you and me?"

"Because she has some things she wants to teach you, and despite my feelings right now, I can't forget what you did in the shower, or in my office. You need to learn self-control and gain my trust again. Do this for me," Clara said. "Please."

Jacob grumbled despite remembering how hot he thought Jackie was the first time he met her. Part of him wanted to fool around with Jackie, but after his emotional roller coaster the last couple of days, Jacob felt out of his element. Normally the idea of wild sex romps would be exciting for him, but right now he just wanted to crawl into bed beside Clara and go to sleep.

"For you then," Jacob agreed. "But I want to register an official request."

Clara smirked. "An official request, huh? And what would that be?"

"After Jackie is done with me, I get one last session with you."

"I think I can arrange that," Clara offered. "But be warned, Jackie is a demanding woman. You had better please her and if I hear otherwise—"

"You won't. I promise. I'll be on my best behavior."

"What was it I said to you about making promises, young man?"

Jacob unfolded his arms and embraced her. Clara was momentarily startled by his swiftness and strength as he drew her into him. She smiled and closed her eyes. He was a fine young man, she thought, with just a few minor faults to still iron out.

"Where is Jackie now? I feel like a stud asking about my next client."

Clara held him for a moment longer than broke the embrace. "She's waiting for you in my bedroom."

"She is?" Jacob turned and glanced into the hallway. "So that's why you stopped me. I guess it would have been a bit of a shock seeing her on your bed waiting for me."

"Remember, Jacob, that this will be hard for me too. Part of me doesn't want to share you anymore, with anyone. But I want to make you a better man—"

"And boyfriend?"

"Don't rush things, Sweetie. I'll be downstairs. You had better impress her and do whatever she commands. And I promise she is well aware you're a virgin, and that you want to save it for someone special."

"Aww, you told her?" Jacob winced. "She's going to think I'm all thumbs."

"She's my best friend. Do a good job impressing her, and I promise that I'll take your virginity. Trust me, I want to be your first."

Hearing those words made Jacob's cock start to rise. He looked down in consternation. "Oh no, I'm sorry. Quick, get the cage before it's too late!"

Clara could barely contain her laughter as Jacob hastily tried to force his growing cock into the small opening of the chastity device. When he gave up in, despair she only shook her head, barely able to contain herself.

"I'll tell Jackie you're having technical difficulties and leave this to you," Clara said as she patted his arm and walked into the hallway.

Jacob felt flustered and watched her disappear with a twinkle of laughter in her wake. While sitting on the bed, he thought of baseball. Sometimes his cock had a mind of its own.

* * *

"He's having trouble with what?" Jackie asked when Clara informed her of Jacob's growing problem.

"He's having some trouble getting the cock cage on," Clara said suppressing a grin and failing. "I might have accidentally aroused him."

"Accidentally?"

"It's not my fault he's in love with me. He shouldn't be too long, though, so I'll leave you two alone," Clara said. She felt thoughts and feelings bubbling to the surface that gave her pause and made her question her decision to punish Jacob at all. Was it jealousy she felt? Jealousy knowing that Jackie would be enjoying Jacob now? Jackie wouldn't steal Jacob from her, would she? Was it fair now to take back her offer to share? No. She could trust Jackie. So long as Jackie didn't take his virginity, then Clara could live with knowing they fooled around. Besides, Clara reasoned, she didn't own Jacob. Not yet, anyway.

Jackie seemed to read her face. "Are you sure you're okay with this?"

"Oh yeah, no problem. I was just making sure I hadn't forgotten anything. So you're all set?"

Jackie looked at her for a moment longer and then seemed satisfied. She looked around the bedroom and nodded. "I think I should be. I just hope you didn't arouse him too much, I don't like waiting."

"Just be sure you don't make the poor boy suffer too much. Remember Jacob hasn't had an orgasm in three days, so you'll probably be working on a hair trigger cock," Clara said.

"Didn't he just cum with Tiffany?"

Clara shook her head. "I'll tell you all about it later, but no, he hasn't yet."

"I'll be careful."

"And make sure he has an orgasm before locking him up again. I plan on making him wait at least a week before I let him out."

"A week?" Jackie shook her head. "You're so cruel. Why a week?"

"If he can show self-control for a week, then I'll be impressed and reward him. A week without an orgasm would be a huge step for him. In the meantime, make him suffer tonight, maybe give him a ruined orgasm or something, but make sure he has some release. Whatever you do, please don't get my sheets sticky. Okay?"

"I think I can work within those boundaries. Now, go away. I need to get my game face on, and decide this boy's fate," Jackie said.

As Clara turned to leave, Jacob appeared in her bedroom doorway. He had managed to attach the cock cage, and he didn't look happy about it.

"Oh, that reminds me," Clara said. She fished out the golden key and tossed it to Jackie. "You might need this."

Jackie snatched the key in the air and palmed it. "Thanks."

Clara gazed at Jacob as she passed him, running her finger up his arm to his shoulder. He looked handsome. Clara had no doubt Jackie would thoroughly enjoy him. That familiar jealousy flared for a moment, but Clara ignored it. She smiled at Jacob, and his forlorn expression brightened.

"Have fun, and remember what I said," Clara whispered in his ear. "I'll be downstairs with headphones on."

Jacob half turned to watch Clara disappear down the hallway. Then, taking a deep breath, he looked at Jackie and walked into the room.

"Close the door, big boy," Jackie said with a mischevious grin. She liked the startled look on his face and admired his muscular body when he turned and closed the bedroom door. "Wow, I'm impressed, young man."

"With what, Mistress?" Jacob asked. He decided to play cautiously with Jackie; she was a much more experienced woman than Tiffany was and probably more cunning and devious. She had propped herself on Clara's four-post bed and looked delicious wearing a skin tight black lycra skirt, black strapped high heels and a pink dress shirt with the top three buttons undone to reveal her ample cleavage.

"I'm impressed with how physically fit you are. Look at you, all muscled and tanned. Clara has been naughty keeping a fine young man like you all to herself. But don't you worry, I plan on tasting your charms," Jackie said.

"You do?" Once more, Jacob felt his cock rise to the occasion, painfully filling the confined space of his chastity device. As his eyes gazed over Jackie's body, he couldn't help but feel his excitement grow.

"Oh, yes. I haven't seen a body like yours for a long, long time."

"What would you command of me?" Jacob said surprised how easily he was slipping into his role-playing persona of a submissive man slave.

Sitting up, Jackie swung her body around on the bed and placed her feet on the floor. She tapped her high heels together and leaned back.

"You can start by taking off my shoes and kissing my feet, you unworthy little man," Jackie said slipping into her persona of the dominant female.

Jacob nodded and moved into a kneeling position on the floor. Jackie offered one foot, and he gently undid the strap of her shoe before pulling it off her heel and setting it on the floor. He then cupped her calf and raised her leg while bending down and kissing the top of her foot. Jackie didn't withdraw her leg, so he continued to plant kisses. After a moment she offered her other shoe, and he repeated the process.

"Beg me to use you, slave," Jackie ordered.

Jacob's cock was throbbing hard, his balls aching from the pressure. He peered into her blue eyes and pleaded. He didn't release her leg and started to slide his tanned, muscular hand up and down her calf enjoying the roundness of it.

"Have you ever given a woman pleasure with your mouth?" Jackie asked nodding towards her privates. "Down there?"

"No, Mistress I have not," Jacob replied with a raised eyebrow. He always wanted to try it, but Katie would never have gone for that, so he never asked.

Pulling her leg from his caressing hands, Jackie frowned. "Crawl over to that water bowl and drink like the dog you are," she said pointing towards Clara's dresser and the small stainless steel bowl she had placed earlier.

Jacob turned and peered at the metal bowl. *Crawl?* He guessed he could do that. Getting down on all fours, he crawled to the bowl. When he arrived, he shot Jackie a quick glance. She was watching him with a smirk on her face and impatiently motioned for him to drink. He took the bowl in his hands, but a sharp *tsk* from Jackie caused him to look at her again.

"Like a dog does it."

Jacob felt his face flush. He set the bowl down and lowered his face to the water. Because he had disturbed it, the water in the bowl got his nose wet. Tilting his head to the side, he tried lapping and slurping the water. It was cool and refreshing, and he enjoyed having a quick drink. Not sure if he was supposed to drink all the water or just some water, he stopped when he felt he had enough and looked back at Jackie.

"Now crawl back and undress me," Jackie ordered.

As Jacob made his way back across the floor, Jackie stood and waited. When he thought he was close enough, Jacob stopped crawling and cautiously stood.

"Come closer. Take off my shirt first."

"Yes, Mistress," Jacob said. He stepped closer and noticed the mirth in her eye as he reached for the hem of her shirt.

"Start with the buttons," Jackie barked, slapping his hands.

Jacob fumbled for the buttons, feeling foolish. He plucked each one in turn until her pink shirt opened and revealed her incredible breasts cupped in a lace bra. He gently peeled back the fabric, and Jackie slowly pulled her arms out and raised her hands over her head. With her shirt off, Jacob's arms stopped moving, and he stared open mouthed at her huge breasts.

Jackie cleared her throat impatiently.

"Oh, I'm sorry," Jacob said barely able to take his eyes off her chest. He had never seen such heavy full breasts except online.

"My eyes are up here," Jackie said in a flat tone.

Jacob tore his eyes away and looked into her eyes. They were the most spectacular breasts he had ever seen, and he wanted to ask if they were real, but chose to remain silent. If Jackie's plan was to act like Clara and Tiffany had during one of these sessions, he knew she would react negatively to any unwanted questions. If he didn't please her, then Jackie would probably deny him permission to fondle her breasts.

"Yes, they are real," Jackie said.

Jacob blinked in surprise. "I didn't ask anything."

"Your eyes did. All men react the same way the first time they see my tits. Yes, they are real. Would you like to touch them?"

Jacob reached up, but Jackie quickly swatted his hands away.

"I only asked a question. I didn't give permission. Take off my skirt," Jackie commanded as she reached behind her back and undid her bra.

"Slave apologizes, Mistress," Jacob said in a whisper. He knelt on one knee and carefully slipped his fingers over her waistband and tugged the skin tight skirt downward. He gasped in shock when he saw she wasn't wearing any panties, but continued to work her skirt down until it was around her ankles.

She placed a hand on his shoulder and stepped out of them and then dropped her bra on the floor. "Stand up."

Jacob rose to his feet, his eyes lingering on her bare breasts as they passed his eyes. His balls ached once more from the pressure of his straining erection. Jackie walked a slow circle, her eyes appraising his body.

"Hold still and do not move," Jackie said and placed her hands on his shoulders. She let her hands wander and slide over his tanned skin, feeling his hard muscles and enjoying it. She continued her slow circle, feeling his biceps, and forearms, then his hard chest and rippling her fingers over his washboard abs. She couldn't recall the last time she had the pleasure of touching such a well formed male body. Perhaps it was in college, she mused, but her memory was foggy. Perhaps she had never been this close to such a perfect male form. Lately, the men she had bedded were older and flabbier, or just plain drab compared to the young man in her possession now. No wonder Clara was so smitten with him and so willing to put the time and effort into turning him into a better man. To her, Jacob looked like the type of guy who might dabble in modeling eventually or be discovered by a talent agent and star in the next blockbuster superhero movie.

She noticed his straining cock and felt pity. The golden key was lying on the sheets, and she deftly scooped it. With the key in hand, she knelt in front of Jacob. He hadn't moved. He was like a monolithic statue, except instead of bronze, he was tanned muscle. Undoing the lock on his cock cage, Jackie removed the device and tossed it aside, and then gasped in pleasant shock as his freed cock grew, and grew and then grew some more until it stood rigid and fully erect.

"Is that better?" Jackie managed to ask.

Jacob nodded, the slightest of grins appearing on his handsome face.

"Don't you dare pull a stunt on me like you did with Clara in the shower," Jackie warned, and she meant it.

Did she know about that too? Jacob's smile vanished. Of course, Clara would have told her best friend. That incident in the shower seemed so long ago, though, and he wouldn't dream of making that kind of mistake again. His thoughts were interrupted when he felt Jackie's hands wrap themselves around his shaft. She had his full attention.

"Such a nice cock," Jacie observed, giving it a few strokes.

"Thank you, Mistress," Jacob said. "It's yours to enjoy."

Jackie suppressed a giggle but inside she doubted he knew what those words did to her already moist pussy. "Oh, is it now? Is this cock somehow yours to offer me? I think not." Her hand gripped harder. "It is mine to take because I own it. You cannot offer me what is mine already."

Jacob understood and nodded while keeping his eyes staring straight ahead.

"If you manage to please me, which I doubt, I might reward you with a proper orgasm. Displease me in any way, even the slightest, and I will give you a ruined orgasm, or no orgasm at all. Do you understand?"

"Yes, Mistress," Jacob said. He felt nervous and eager at the same time.

Jackie released his cock and reclined on the bed, propping her shoulders on a pillow and drawing her knees up. She motioned for Jacob to get on the bed, and he did.

"One skill every man should develop is the ability to please a woman with oral sex," Jackie said. She spread her knees apart revealing her smoothly shaven pussy. Jacob shivered with anticipation as he gazed at her splendor.

"Teach me how to do it, please."

"Oh, I intend to. First, lie down on your stomach. Get nice and close and start gently kissing all around. Remember it's like a petal and needs to be treated softly. Rush in like a horny dog and the petals close. Access denied. The secret to pleasing a woman and opening her petals is being able to build the heat slowly. You may begin."

Jacob appreciated her advice and moved his head between her legs. He gazed at her soft white skin and gently kissed her inner thigh. It was soft and smooth. He nibbled little kisses towards her pussy, stopping just short. Looking at a vagina this close was a new experience for him, and he breathed in her musky scent. Without realizing it, his hips ground into the mattress. He turned his head to her other thigh and kissed her there too. Jackie responded with a purr and encouraging sounds.

"Very nice start," she said. "Now put your lips on it and let your tongue explore. No need to rush, just enjoy the feeling."

Jacob gave her a short nod and lowered his mouth to her clit. His heart was racing with excitement. He had never observed the delicate beauty of a woman's vagina before, and it intrigued him. He kissed her swollen folds and then slipped his tongue out. She was warm and tasted slightly metallic. Jackie responded immediately to his tender passion by running her hands through his thick hard hair. Growing bolder, Jacob stuck his tongue between her folds again and licked her pussy from bottom to top. Jackie cooed, and a soft moan escaped her mouth.

"Now keep going in that area and don't stop until I tell you to."

Jacob felt encouraged by her words and continued. He wasn't sure he was doing it right. He read her body language to determine what was working and what wasn't; it was as good a road map as any. It didn't take long for Jackie's juices to start flowing and soon Jacob's face and lips were glistening and wet.

Arching her back, Jackie let the sensations of his handsome mouth ripple through her body. She ran her hands through his hair again and gripped his head gently, guiding and directing his mouth over her clit. She couldn't recall the last time a man went down on her. It had to have been at least a decade when she was in her early twenties. Men nowadays seldom pleasure a woman orally, and Jackie missed it. She directed his mouth to her clit and held him there as her warm juices started to churn. She felt waves of pleasure slowly building and building. His muscular arms cradled her ass as he forced his tongue deeper into her warmth, flicking and licking all around.

Unable to take any more, Jackie gasped and quivered. She tensed and clenched her pussy muscles as her orgasm crashed over her like a warm ocean current. Jacob, unaware that she was cumming continued to work his mouth, making her climax even stronger. She gripped his head and bucked her hips, forcing her pussy to grind his face while her long legs wrapped around his torso and held him in place. As her orgasm blissfully faded, Jackie moaned in content satisfaction.

"How did I do?" Jacob asked, his head popping up from between her legs. His lips and face were covered in her slippery juices, but he didn't mind at all.

"You may stop now," Jackie said with a smile. "Well done for your first time. Did you enjoy it?"

Jacob licked his lips. "That was incredible."

Jackie laughed. "Well if you liked it so much, perhaps you could do that again for me another time."

"Yes please."

"One word of advice if you are ever going to do this for another woman, though. Make sure she is freshly showered and thoroughly clean like I was. It will make the whole experience so much better."

"Note taken, Mistress. I loved that."

"I'm glad. Now lie down on your back, head on the pillows. It's time for some more fun," Jackie said, still reeling from her powerful orgasm. In her mind, Jacob was a keeper just for his sheer eagerness. Jacob moved from between her legs allowing Jackie to roll off the bed and compose herself.

"On the edge or in the middle?" Jacob asked.

"In the middle. Arms and legs spread eagle," Jackie replied. Her legs felt weak.

Jacob rolled onto his back and moved to the center of the bed. He watched with eager eyes as Jackie produced two pairs of handcuffs and four coils of soft black nylon rope. First Jackie slapped cuffs around each of his wrists and then looped the rope through them. She then attached each rope to opposite bedposts and drew his arms wide before tying heavy knots. With the remaining two coils, she wrapped each of his ankles leaving enough left over to reach the bottom bedposts where she once again made heavy knots.

"You've done this before I take it?" Jacob asked, surprised at how efficiently she had secured him to the bed.

"I've done this a few times, but trust me, I'm not a professional yet."

"Yet?"

"Regardless, I think you look pretty stuck. Can you move? How's the circulation? I always worry I make my knots too tight."

Jacob laughed. "I'm getting used to this you know." He tested each limb against the bindings and then looked at Jackie. "I think I'm snug."

"Great, now for the next part of our little session I'm going to enjoy myself. I don't want you speaking or talking or making any comments. Your job is to lie there and be quiet."

He had heard the words *be quiet* before and understood perfectly. Before these sessions, he never would have guessed how annoyed women became if you talked during sex. Not that he had much experience with sex, but he couldn't understand what it was about hearing a man talk that annoyed women so much.

Straddling his torso on all fours, Jackie peered in Jacob's hapless face and licked her lips. Part of her had to admit she enjoyed having control over a man and seeing such a fine example of a man under her control made her excitement even greater. Bending her arms, Jackie lowered her face towards his. When he lifted his head to kiss her, Jackie pulled back in annoyance.

"Did I give you permission to kiss me?" Jackie whispered.

"No."

"Then don't. I told you to hold still and not move."

"Yes, Mistress."

Jackie lowered her head once more, her eyes watching carefully for any movement before she nestled her nose into his neck. She could detect a faint trace of his aftershave or cologne and thought it was a good scent. His body was warm, and his muscles taut and hard. Her pussy tingled with anticipation. Unfortunately, she would have to wait until after Jacob lost his virginity to Clara before riding him. She had promised Clara, and she intended to keep that promise.

Kissing the nape of his neck, Jackie worked across his chest until she paused and gently touched his trembling lips with hers.

She liked his lips, and his kisses were warm, so she allowed him to return the favor for a moment before breaking away and smiling. Jackie began to kiss her way down his chest but then stopped suddenly. Jacobs' eyes went wide as his erect cock poked Jackie's pussy while she was moving down. Jackie gasped and quickly reversed her body.

"Oops," Jackie blushed. "Not used to cocks that stand on their own. Sorry."

"Did it go in?" Jacob asked with a horrified expression.

Placing a hand on his sculpted chest, Jackie chuckled. "Don't you worry, it wasn't even close. Clara tells me she is looking forward to riding your big hard cock. Is that true?"

Jacob relaxed, his worried expression melting into chagrin. "I want her to be my first."

"Why?" Jackie asked, suddenly curious.

"I've never met a woman like her. She's perfect. Everything about her is perfect. I want my first time to be special. Promise not to laugh."

Jackie smiled at his earnestness. "I wouldn't laugh at that."

"Thank you," Jacob whispered.

Moving between his spread legs, Jackie knelt so her her face was close to his erect and throbbing cock, her blue eyes examining every inch of him. She wrapped a hand around his base and felt the strong muscles in his cock flex. He was impressive, she thought. Not many men have both length and girth, and some men have just one or the other, while some poor souls have neither. Jacob, she thought, was blessed with a great cock.

"I like your cock," Jackie said.

Lifting his head, Jacob peered at her with a bewildered expression.

"Um, thanks, I guess."

"No, I mean it, you have a great cock. Women would kill to fuck a cock like this. Clara is going to love it. If I hadn't promised Clara not to, I would ride you for hours. I know how to keep a man hard for a very long time if I wanted. But a promise is a promise," Jackie said in a wistful tone. She moved her fingers up and down his cock admiring it more.

"I'm sorry," Jacob offered. "I want Clara to be my first."

"Don't be sorry. Another time maybe. Clara and I share a lot," Jackie said but stopped short of mentioning other men. There was no need to tarnish his image of Clara.

"Really?"

"If Clara is willing to share you some more," Jackie replied. She tilted his cock towards her mouth and licked the tip. "Then I would be a fool to turn down this gorgeous dick."

Jacob set his head back on the pillow and stared at the ceiling. He was thinking about Clara again. Jackie guessed where his thoughts were, but she wasn't offended. Part of her wished she had a guy who looked at her the way Jacob looked at Clara. Jackie took his cock into her mouth and started gently sucking. He smiled and closed his eyes.

It didn't take long for Jacob to nearly orgasm. Jackie stopped in mid stroke, her mouth sensing that familiar convulsion all cocks have just before they start to spurt. She carefully took him out of her mouth and gently laid his cock against his belly and backed away. Any stimulation could set him off. She watched carefully, wondering if she stopped too late. His cock convulsed, lifted up slightly and then fell back down and was still.

"Why did you stop?" Jacob breathed in exasperation. He was peering at her now, his brow furrowed and his face a mask of confusion.

Jackie frowned right back. "I thought I told you not to speak. Clara was right; you don't know how to listen very well."

"Argh, I can't take this!" Jacob grunted in frustration and slammed his head into the pillow. "I was so close!" He took long breaths and squeezed his eyes shut. Jackie waited. She had no choice; she had to let his orgasm subside. When he opened his eyes, he was cool, calm and collected.

"Better now?" Jackie asked in an amused tone.

"Slave is sorry, Mistress."

"Much better," Jackie said. She crossed her arms on his legs and watched with fascination as Jacob's cock calmed down. After a few minutes, Jackie gently picked up his dying cock and stroked it back to life. Jacob tensed as new sensations flooded his body. He pulled against the restraints on his wrists and ankles and bucked his hips, but this only made Jackie laugh. His fading orgasm did a quick reversal, this time building much faster.

Just as before, Jackie could feel his cock begin to convulse and immediately stopped stroking him. She rested his aching shaft against his tummy once again, folded her arms and waited.

Jacob moaned and tried to buck his hips in frustration, his head turning every which way on the pillow. When she glanced at his face, she was pleased to see a tormented expression. She suspected this was Jacob's first experience with edging. It could be torturous for a man and last for as long as a woman desires.

"Please..." Jacob whispered. His brow was sweaty.

"I thought Clara taught you that your cock isn't there for your pleasure. Your cock is mine to use as I see fit, and right now I'm enjoying edging you a little. Yes, I suppose this is frustrating, but deal with it. I will do as I please."

A soft whimper was Jacob's only reply.

Jackie had to wait longer the second time she edged him for his cock to calm down enough that she could touch it. There comes a point just before a man has an orgasm where if you stop just a tad late, the orgasm continues its own. She always thought of this as the "oh-oh" moment and had experienced it many times before she perfected her edging technique. It's the point in which there is nothing you can do to stop a man from blowing his load. The trick, she discovered over the years, is to stop just before the "oh-oh" moment, unless you wanted to give a man a ruined orgasm. That was simple. Just bring him to the "oh-oh" moment and then one stroke more before backing off. She often enjoyed seeing men squirm as their orgasms sputtered and she savored the sound of men in pleasure-denying cries of agony. But if you want to prolong the fun, edging was the most fun thing to do to a tied man. And Jackie wanted to prolong her fun.

"You have no idea how horny playing with your cock is making me," Jackie said as she slipped her hand between her silky thighs.

Jacob lifted his head, his exasperated eyes blinking and unfocused. He stared at Jackie and saw no pity in her expression. His head fell back onto the pillow, and he groaned. He was going to be denied an orgasm for quite a while it appeared.

"Can we do three times? Let's try," Jackie said in a playful voice.

"Please let me cum," Jacob whispered. When she grabbed his cock once more, he flexed his strength against the bindings in frustration.

Opening her mouth, Jackie slipped his thick cock between her lips and flicked her tongue on the underside. She wasn't sure how many times, if ever, Jacob had been given a blowjob. Regardless of the number, Jackie wanted to be sure her performance would be the one all others were compared to and found wanting.

Working her hand up and down his shaft, stroking and twisting in unison with her bobbing head, Jackie went to work. She teased and pulled and sucked and tickled, taking him deeper and deeper into her mouth until eventually, she was slipping his shaft past the back of her throat.

Jacob had stopped struggling and peered in awe. He watched his cock disappear nearly all the way into Jackie's mouth and down her throat. He had seen this happen in porn movies but never in a million years would imagine it was happening to him. The sensations were incredible, and he willed her to go faster.

Jackie's eyes watered a little, but she was fine with runny mascara. She relaxed her gag reflex and worked his cock all the way in, pressing her nose against his body. She held him there, feeling his thick shaft press against the sides of her throat. The sensation of suffocating was normal, and she controlled her urge to pull back. She held herself steady, moving her tongue around to stimulate the base of his shaft. Then she slowly and deliberately pulled her head back, feeling the thickness of his cock sliding out of her throat. Refilling her lungs, Jackie smiled at Jacob's stunned expression and jerked his wet cock in her hand.

"How was that?"

Jacob opened his mouth, but no words came out. He just blinked and stared in amazement.

"Let's see if we can almost cum again," Jackie said. She loved edging men and seeing the sexual torment on their faces. She was impressed that she managed to bring Jacob to the edge of orgasm twice already. Having so much control over Jacob's pleasure made Jackie even wetter.

"Please let me cum," Jacob begged.

"We'll see," Jackie said in a tone that told him there was little hope. She gripped his cock harder and cupped his balls, massaging and stroking his helpless shaft. Jacob grunted and tried to buck his hips, but nothing he did slowed Jackie's persistent stroking. She twisted her stroke making sure she went from the base of his shaft all the way to the tip and backed down again. His orgasm started to build almost immediately. Three days of not doing what he did every day of his life must have been a big shock to his system, Jackie thought. Now with her edging session, poor Jacob must be in absolute agony. She grinned and stroked faster.

"Oh look at that, I think your cock is about to cum. I can't wait to see all that hot cum cover my tits. Oh, please Jacob, cum on me, I need it," Jackie taunted, enjoying how Jacob's face contorted as his balls started to twitch.

She could feel his orgasm about to come and stopped. She set his cock down and watched. It convulsed and spasmed. Jacob groaned and nearly howled in frustration. Pre-cum dripped from the tip of his cock onto his belly, but his orgasm wouldn't follow.

"I'm impressed, Jacob. Three edgings without an orgasm. How does it feel to want something so badly and be so close, only to be denied by a woman?"

"It's terrible! Please just jerk me off."

"What fun would that be? Once you men blow your loads, you always lose interest and want to sleep. A woman has to take charge to make sure she is satisfied first. Hasn't Clara taught you that?"

Jacob relented in frustration, turning his head away he suffered in silence.

Pleased with herself, Jackie opened her purse and pulled out her favorite sex toy; a thick silicone cock. She liked this one in particular because it had a wide suction-cup base. Straddling Jacob's chest, she waited until his eyes turned and looked at her. He was raging with lust and Jackie loved it. She placed one knee under his armpit, and a foot beside his head, so her pussy was in full view of his hungry eyes. Without saying a word she reached between her legs and pulled her swollen lips apart and wiggled the head of the toy cock against her opening. With little movements back and forth, Jackie let her wet juices lubricate the toy.

"Oh no, I don't think I can take more of this," Jacob said. "First Tiffany and then you. Please, I'm so damn horny. Just make me cum now, please!"

"Not until I'm satisfied," Jackie replied. The silicone cock didn't take long to become slippery, and she adjusted her position to make sure she was right over Jacob's face, his eyes only inches from her wet snatch.

The sensations that her toy created were intense. The toy cock always brought her pleasure but masturbating above Jacob's helpless face is what gave her pleasure that extra zing. Grabbing the rubber cock with both hands, Jackie pressed her heavy breasts together with her arms and began to pump her pussy.

Jacob felt like his cock was going to explode. He had never felt so aroused in all his life, and there was absolutely nothing stimulating his cock. He hungered for her big breasts and imagined grabbing her roughly and flipping her over on the stomach and ramming his cock deep into her ass, but he couldn't do any of that. He pulled the restraints helplessly feeling his frustration grow even more.

The power she held over him was intoxicating, and Jackie began to cry out in pleasure. Her voice rose higher as she pumped the toy in and out faster and faster until her orgasm crested and she nearly tumbled over. Her pussy contracted and clenched and squeezed every sensation out of the buried toy. She gulped in air and convulsed as her powerful orgasm washed over her.

"Oh god, that was amazing!" Jackie said as she laid down on the bed ignoring Jacob's flustered agonized face.

"It certainly was," Clara said from the doorway. Jacob's head swiveled, and his eyes pleaded with hope.

Jackie propped her body on an elbow and laughed. "You dirty whore, how long have you been watching me?"

"Long enough to be wet and horny," Clara said as she walked to the edge of the bed. She glanced at Jacob's throbbing trigger happy cock and then at his tormented face.

"Please, Clara..."

"Hush up you," Clara said.

"He still hasn't learned a thing," Jackie observed. "So what brings you up here? Looking to join the festivities?"

Clara bit her lip and gently stroked Jacob's cock. "I just couldn't wait any longer. Knowing Tiffany was playing with Jacob, and then you, well I just got so horny being all alone." She peered into Jacob's eyes while still gently stroking his cock. "You don't mind, honey if I come and play a little too?"

"I don't mind!" Jacob said in a rush of excitement.

"What did you have in mind?" Jackie asked. She placed her hand around Jacob's cock as well, adding her grip to Clara's. They gently stroked him in unison starting off with slow, deliberate movements.

"I'm not sure," Clara said, stroking his cock with a tighter grip.

Jacob moaned.

"Have you come here to take his virginity?" Jackie asked innocently as she increased the pace of her hand forcing Clara to increase her pace too.

"You think I should?" Clara asked thoughtfully. "I don't know if I should, I mean he's such a young man." She matched Jackie's strokes and then pushed her faster.

Jacob nodded, but neither woman looked at him.

"He does have a very nice cock," Jackie observed as she cupped Jacob's balls.

"You're right," Clara said. Together with Jackie, she stroked even faster now, their paired hands working in frenzied unison. "I would love this cock deep inside me."

"If he cums before you're ready, then I guess he'll have to wait for another day," Jackie observed leaning forward and adding her second hand to Jacob's cock.

"You're right," Clara said. She added her extra hand as well. "If he cums, then his cock is no use to us. I wanted to feel his big cock deep in my wet pussy and let him cum in me."

Jacob clenched his teeth and fought his urge to cum but four hands stroking him off without mercy was too much. It was a losing battle.

"Well, I was hoping to let him cum on my tits and all over my face," Jackie said with a sly grin. "But you're right, if he cums, none of that could happen."

"Don't cum, Jacob," Clara said with a wicked grin. Her two hands plus Jackie's two hands worked his shaft relentlessly. She was surprised he lasted this long, but there was no escape for Jacob. They would stroke him off until he could fight no more.

Jacob's face turned red as he fought to contain his orgasm but he couldn't prevent his overly aroused cock from being stroked. He cried out in frustration as his balls contracted and his cock began to convulse.

Clara and Jackie glanced at each other and smiled. Without a word both women stopped their hands and spread their fingers around the base of his cock supporting it upright and waited.

Jacob's body heaved against the bindings, and he lifted his upper body off the bed in a half-situp as his cock began to spurt heavy thick ropes of cum. It was a violent orgasm, and Jackie flinched in surprise. Clara felt pity and moved her hand to grip his shaft. He didn't deserve another ruined orgasm, but Jackie tapped her wrist and shook her head. Clara bit her lip with an uncertain nod and moved her hand away.

"You tricked me!" Jacob cried. "How was I supposed to resist that?"

"Did you have fun?" Clara asked.

Jacob found it difficult to speak, but he managed a nod though he would have preferred to have lost his virginity to Clara instead of being jerked off. Still, it was a release his cock had been aching for none-the-less.

"Look at this mess," Clara said as she lifted her cum covered hands and arms. Jackie laughed and held up her splattered hands. It appeared that neither of them had escaped.

"I need a shower, I think," Jacob said quietly.

A shower?

Jackie glanced at Clara with a raised eyebrow and a smirk. Clara thought for a moment then nodded. The idea had the possibility, she mused. Jackie broke into a smile.

"Do you think it's safe to shower with him?" Clara asked.

"Only if he promises to behave," Jackie said in a firm voice. "Would you like to shower with two naked women, Jacob?"

"Is this a test?"

Clara laughed at his question and helped Jackie remove Jacob's restraints. She leaned closer and kissed his cheek. "Of course, sweetheart. Everything's a test."

"You know," Jackie said as she tapped her cheek with a finger. "We should make him clean all this up and put everything away. That's not our job."

Clara glanced at Jacob and caught his uncertain eye. "You're right, of course. Man slave, clean all this up, and the stuff in Katie's room. Jackie and I are going to relax and have a drink."

"You are?" Jacob asked.

"Clean all this up, then get in the shower and wash-up. When we decide to join you, I expect your body to be glistening clean. Is that understood?" Clara said.

Grumbling silently, Jacob nodded. He wanted to shower off; his body was coated in sweat and his semen, but once again, Clara and Jackie were making demands. Part of him was hurt that they forced him to orgasm even though they both knew he desperately wanted to have sex for the first time instead.

* * *

"I think I hear the shower running," Jackie said twenty minutes later as she tilted her head. She was in the kitchen enjoying a fine glass of white wine.

Clara set her glass down and listened for a moment. "Yup, I guess he cleaned up. Should we go up now?"

Jackie took another sip. "Why rush? That boy will wait. Enjoy your wine. Besides, this gives him a little time to recuperate."

Clara liked the sound of that. "So we're going to play with him more?"

"Of course, girl. Don't be silly. You don't let a man like that out of your grasp until he's wrung every orgasm from your body first. I don't know about you, but I could use two or three more."

"You are such a whore!" Clara teased. "I'd settle for one more orgasm."

Jackie was sipping her wine again, her blue eyes watching Clara with amusement. She swirled her wine a little. "Are you still planning on making him wait a whole week?"

"I am. It's Jacob's final test. One week in the cock cage with no release. If he can do that, I will reward him."

"Don't you think you've tortured him enough? Just fuck him today and get it over with."

Clara shook her head. "I want it to be special, and I want him to learn some self-control. If I give in now, it looks like I'm too eager."

"Suit yourself," Jackie said. "I'd totally fuck him today. We can still play in the shower if he's up to it?"

Finishing the last of her wine, Clara stood and gazed towards the stairs. "I sure hope so."

Jackie polished off her drink and followed Clara up the stairs.

When they strode into Clara's room, both women glanced towards the shower. The water was on, and thick billows of steam were already obscuring their view of Jacob. Giving Clara a wink, Jackie started to peel off her clothes. Just as eagerly, Clara disrobed as well. She felt nervous and excited at the same time.

"Shall we enjoy ourselves?" Jackie asked gesturing towards the shower.

"We most certainly shall," Clara replied with a lick of her lips.

Together, the two naked women sauntered into the mist.

Jacob wasn't aware that the two of them were there until the clear glass door opened. He had been standing with his eyes closed under the hot water letting it soak into his sore shoulder muscles. When he heard the glass door latch, he opened his eyes and beheld the most beautiful sight her had ever seen. No one spoke a word. They didn't need to. He smiled at Clara and offered his hand. When she took it, he closed his fingers and pulled her into him. Her eyes drew wide momentarily, but when he wrapped an arm around her shoulder and held her close, she put a hand on his chest and nestled into him. Jackie put an arm around his shoulder and snuggled her breasts into him before tilting her head for a kiss. Jacob obliged and discovered Jackie was a very good kisser. A small sound from Clara broke his concentration and then her hand gently grabbed his chiseled jaw and turned his head towards her. With a hungry look in her eye, Clara locked her lips on Jacob's. He soon forgot about Jackie and turned his attention to Clara. He gently cupped her face in his hands and admired the woman he had loved for so long. Their eyes found each other and for a moment neither moved as water trickled and splashed around them. Then tilting her head back, Jacob began to kiss her again. Jackie stood close, her eyes filling with lust as she ran her hands up and down both Clara and Jacob's slippery backs. She enjoyed watching them kiss.

After a little while, Jacob reached for Jackie and drew her closer too. The three of them hugged and snuggled under the water and yet no one spoke. Jacob suddenly smirked and turned Clara and Jackie's faces towards each other motioning them to kiss. Both women grinned and embraced each other, planting soft passionate kisses while Jacob watched with fascination. His hands found Clara's breasts, and he lovingly caressed them, while his other hand groped Jackie's much larger breasts. Neither woman complained nor said a word, so he continued a little longer. Stepping back he grabbed one of Clara's scented body wash bottles and squeezed some soap into his hand. He then stepped behind Clara and gently started lathering her backside and shoulders. He then moved behind Jackie and did the same. Refilling his palm with more soap, he reached between the kissing women and started to lather their breasts. His cock was stiff again, but he ignored it and focussed on tending to the two naked goddesses with him.

Clara and Jackie finally separated, and they smiled at him and continued where he left off, slathering their bodies and each other. When they finished, Jackie glanced at Jacob and then at Clara with a raised eyebrow. Clara giggled and grabbed the bottle of body wash while Jackie backed Jacob against the tiled wall. She intertwined her fingers with his and lifted his hands over his head and pinned them against the wall. Jacob was intrigued and watched eagerly.

Stepping closer, Clara began to wash his chest and torso. She often stopped to steal more kisses from Jacob, and he gave them willingly. She washed all the way down to his rock hard cock and then stopped. Jacob looked at her questioningly. Silently, Clara replaced Jackie's interlaced fingers with her own and leaned into him, kissing him deeply while holding his hands pinned. Jackie then squeezed some body wash into her palms and knelt on the floor and lathered each of his legs, working her way up to his throbbing cock. She paused and with soapy hands reached behind him and lathered his tight butt enjoying how muscular it was. With his cock the last part of his body not washed, Jackie grinned and grabbed it. Clara looked down and then up again. She gave him a stern warning look before releasing Jacob's hands from the wall. He knew what she meant and kept them in place. She nodded and then knelt beside Jackie. While Jackie was cleaning his cock, Clara took to washing his balls and working her hands up and down his thighs.

Jacob was enthralled watching the two women take turns stroking and washing his cock. He wasn't nearly as trigger happy this time, but he did feel he could cum again if this continued. Not wanting to ruin the moment by speaking, Jacob gently brushed the eager hands away and turned towards the water to rinse. Both Clara and Jackie seemed surprised and remained kneeling where he left them. They watched him rinse clean, admiring his broad muscular back and tight bottom.

When all the soap was gone, he turned and glanced at the two kneeling women. He slowly approached Jackie and stood in front of her with his hands on his hips and his erect cock pointed at her face. She glanced up in surprise, her blue eyes sparkling. She seemed to consider his unspoken words before opening her mouth. Jacob moved forward slightly and tilted his cock until the head was resting on her bottom lip. He could feel Jackie's hot breath. She took him, slowly at first, enjoying how thick and strong his cock was. Clara moved to the side and watched with fascination. While Jackie's head bobbed and her mouth worked his cock, Jacob offered Clara a hand.

She looked at it before placing her smaller hand in it. He pulled her to her feet and wrapped an arm around her waist yanking her body into his. He then drew his hand up her back and leaned in for a kiss. Clara was breathing hard and found herself kissing him with a hunger she hadn't felt in a long time.

A few minutes later Jacob pulled his head back and looked down at Jackie who was diligently sucking and slurping on his rigid cock. He stepped back a little and Jackie looked up. He thanked her with his eyes and then turned to Clara again. Her cheeks were flushed and her eyes wide, her dark hair matted and plastered to her forehead. He placed hands on her shoulders and gently nudged her down. She understood immediately and knelt on the shower floor.

Jackie began to rub her clit as she watched. Clara grabbed the base of Jacob's cock with both hands and started planting kisses all along the underside of it. She kissed the tip and then opened her mouth and started to suck. Jacob gasped and shut his eyes as pleasure washed over him. He regained his composure and opened them again, eager to watch the most beautiful woman he had ever known suck his cock.

Clara grabbed his cock in one hand and his balls in the other and gently massaged and teased while her mouth worked. She hungrily slurped her tongue flicking and whipping around his shaft without slowing.

It didn't take long, and Jacob felt his orgasm starting. He tapped Clara gently to warn her, and she looked up and him and nodded, then redoubled her efforts. Jacob gasped when he realized she wanted him to cum in her mouth. He tensed his muscles trying to force his orgasm to delay so he could enjoy her blowjob even longer, but Clara was determined and kept going. Finally, he moaned loudly and felt his cock begin to spurt. Clara slowed her sucking and pressed her lips tightly around his shaft. She gently jerked and milked his cock as cum spurted and filled her mouth. He didn't shoot as much cum as earlier, but Clara was certain whatever was left was now drained.

When his cock was done convulsing, Clara still kept her mouth sealed around his shaft. She carefully milked any remaining cum in his spent cock before letting it go. Jacob nearly staggered back, but he was curious what she would do with a mouthful of his semen. Jackie climaxed, her hand rubbing furiously enough to make her firm breasts giggle. Both Jacob and Clara had forgotten about her. Clara waited patiently until Jackie's eyes opened, her cheeks puffed out and little droplets of cum seeping down her chin.

When she was certain she had both Jackie and Jacob's attention, Clara opened her mouth to show both of them how much cum she had collected and then closed her mouth and swallowed. She could feel the whole slippery mess slide down her throat, but she didn't feel disgusted. She felt happy. She knew how much this would mean for Jacob. Triumphantly Clara opened her empty mouth to show what she had done.

Jackie could only stare in amazement. She had never seen Clara do that. In fact, she didn't even know Clara could swallow cum. She often did, so it was no big deal for her, but as far as Jackie knew, Clara had never once done that. She nodded in approval.

Jacob was even more enthralled with Clara now. He offered both women a hand to stand. He was amazed that no one had spoken a word. Clara was about to step under the nozzle when Jacob gently grabbed her forearm. She looked at him and winked. He cupped her chin and kissed her passionately. Jackie could only smile as she stole the water and rinsed herself off. When she was ready to get out, Jackie motioned her intentions to the two love birds, but neither of them noticed. Chuckling to herself, Jackie closed the shower stall behind her and snagged a towel. She quietly left so Jacob and Clara could have a little alone time together.

They didn't come out for another twenty minutes. There was no way either of them would last the week. Jackie was willing to bet money on it.

The End

Printed in Great Britain
by Amazon

29024453R00129